Little Mocker's Great Adventure

Little Mocker was lost. With a broken wing he couldn't fly home – ever if he knew where home was. The animals of the Deep Forest drew near and listened to his story . . .

So began Little Mocker's Great Adventure. As it turned out, it was in adventure for all his new friends – the kindly Mr and Mrs Raccoon; brave Rabbit; Skunky; Dump Pile Rat; Head Frog (who always knew the answer) – and many others.

This delightful tale of Little Mocker's adventures is fresh, funny, unsentimental – and full of surprises.

Little Mocker's Great Adventure

JEAN BELL MOSLEY

Illustrations by Joan Auclair

A LION PAPERBACK
Tring · Batavia · Sydney

Copyright © 1985 Jean Bell Mosley
Illustrations © Joan Auclair

First British edition 1986

Published by
Lion Publishing plc
Icknield Way, Tring, Herts, England
ISBN 0 7459 1200 1
Albatross Books Pty Ltd
PO Box 320, Sutherland, NSW 2232, Australia
ISBN 0 86760 837 4

British Library Cataloguing in Publication Data
Mosley, Jean Bell
  [The deep forest award]. Little Mocker's
  great adventure.
  I. [The deep forest award]   II. Title
  III. Auclair, Joan
  813'.54 [J]   PZ7
  ISBN 0 7459 1200 1

Printed and bound in Great Britain
by Cox & Wyman Ltd, Reading

For
Lauren Patricia Mosley

CONTENTS

1
Noises in the Night

There were three noises that night, all about the same time. A big one went Crack-Splat-Slam-Whomp! A middle-sized one went Rattley-Clang-Bang! A little one went Thud, followed by a faint Gasp, as of something having the breath knocked out of it.

The middle-sized one was at the dump pile. A brightly painted boxlike contraption with brass trimmed corners that had been teetering on the edge of the dump for several days finally slid down the slope of accumulated tin cans, old tyres, broken chairs, sprung springs, perforated pots, and other items too numerous to mention. The jar of the fall caused some coloured lights inside the box to wink and blink and a jumble of sounds to come forth from a little hole in one side. Since no creature was around to hear, not even Dump Pile Rat, he being deep within his castle and fast asleep, this noise was not noticed.

The little Thud-Gasp, a half mile away from the dump, over by the hedgerow, was entirely missed, too.

But the great Crack-Splat-Slam-Whomp! was heard by many.

"What was that?" said Mrs. Raccoon to Mr. Raccoon as they both somersaulted out of bed and landed on the floor halfway across their big white oak bedroom. The little Flower Garden quilt under which they had been so snugly sleeping had risen like a wind-puffed circus tent, floated swiftly overhead, and was now settling softly over them. At first, Mrs. Raccoon thought it a heavenly cloud come to shield them from sights and sounds of a world that must be ending. When her toenails caught in the quilting stitches, which clouds don't have, she knew it was time to be more realistic, ready for action, full of concentration and whatever maximum effort it would take to save them from this monstrous thing that had come like a thief in the night.

"That was a loud noise," said Mr. Raccoon practically, trying to keep from shaking so Mrs. Raccoon wouldn't know how frightened he was. "Only a loud noise," he repeated with much assurance. He waggled his ears, which were uncomfortably bent by the quilt, tweaked his whiskers, and threw the cover aside, prepared to do whatever must be done to protect his home.

"I felt the house shake all over," said Mrs. Raccoon. "Was it thunder?"

"No thunder. No storm," said Mr. Raccoon. "See, moonlight coming in the doorway."

"The hunters?" whispered Mrs. Raccoon. "Do you think they have come to cut down our house? Is this the end?" Tears trickled down her nose and fell on her feet. She wiped them dry on the quilt. Wet feet were fun when paddling around in rivers and brooks, but slick feet were *not* good in an emergency. She looked around as if she might be seeing their home and all its cozy little fitments for the last time.

It was such a nice little home high up in a hole in a white oak tree where they had raised their children, amassed their treasures, and took from everyday living the joys and satisfactions that are always there for those who look and see. It smelled of crushed acorns, fragrant leaves, and bark. Where fungi had made a scallop-edged shelf against the wall, they had arranged their riches. There was the bottom half of a blue Vicks Vapo-rub jar Mr. Raccoon had found at the dump pile, three foil balls of chewing gum wrappers, and twenty-seven can tab openers. They could have had more of the latter, but the very commonness of them now devalued them, and they had decided not to bring home any more—bright, light, and shiny though they be. Their most prized piece was a small tin bucket, also salvaged from the dump pile. Mrs. Raccoon kept rosehips, corn, acorns, pecans, and other assorted nuts in it. The outside was so shiny she sometimes paused to have a look at her ears to see if they were clean inside or count the seven black rings in her tail, a number she had been told was uncommon in the raccoon branch of animalhood.

Now these treasures lay scattered all over the floor. Mrs. Raccoon brushed them aside with her tail and cautioned Mr. Raccoon, "Don't get too close to the doorway. They'll shine a light in your eyes."

"I don't think it is the hunters," said Mr. Raccoon. "Come here and look."

Mrs. Raccoon crept noiselessly across the room to stand beside Mr. Raccoon in their doorway.

"Look at the hedgerow." Mr. Raccoon pointed five fingers at once, which made it difficult for Mrs. Raccoon to pinpoint any certain place. "Do you see anything different?"

Mrs. Raccoon peered out into the night, but not before taking a quick look straight down the trunk of their house to make sure no hunters lurked there with those long sticks that barked fire. Yes, she could see immediately that something appeared different about the landscape. But what was it? She gave the whole L-shaped hedgerow, which bordered two sides of the Grassy Meadow, a quick glance, then began to cover it systematically. Beginning at the far corner where it became a part of the Deep Forest, she let her eyes travel slowly along. There was the wild plum thicket that had earlier made a fragrant white cloud of blossoms. There was the persimmon patch where they'd had family reunions each October. It being a warm spring night, breezes were tilting honeysuckle cups, spilling perfume into the air which mingled with an incredible number of other pleasant springtime smells. She had always loved this view from their round doorway and whenever tired or low-spirited had come to stand there and just look out on the good world. For a moment she forgot that wasn't what she was doing now and was ready to call Mr. Raccoon's attention to the quality of the softly stirring air and how the moonlight on the Rustling Brook that ran through the Grassy Meadow seemed to be making a silver pathway.

But Mr. Raccoon, keeping his mind on the business at hand, interrupted her thinking by saying, "I see.

It is the big dead hickory. It has fallen at last. Look, a part of it has hit our house."

"That's it," said Mrs. Raccoon, relieved. Then, clasping her hands in 'coonly dismay, she said, "Oh my, Woodpecker and her new children were in the hickory. Do you suppose—?" She could not bring herself to finish the question, for she felt a great tenderness for all the creatures of the hills and valleys and rivers and meadows, and although hunger had sometimes forced her to eat an egg now and then, an egg that might have become a bird or a chicken or a duck, she had a mother's heart for the newly hatched or born.

"They left last week," Mr. Raccoon said quickly to comfort his mate. "I'm going down to have a look."

"Oh no, not yet. Let us see if someone else comes first. Dog, for instance." Mr. Raccoon shuddered at the thought, for Dog's coming usually meant trouble. "Maybe Mother 'Possum will come or Rabbit. Rabbit is always Johnny-on-the-spot when anything smacks of trouble. Or Skunky. Yes, wait and let Skunky come first. He's always a sort of—well a sort of—"

"Protective element?" Mr. Raccoon supplied the words, smiling. "Yes, you have to hand it to Skunky. He has his good points in certain circumstances when Dog is around. But I'm going on down. We can't just stand back and not get involved when things like this happen. Who knows—Rabbit, Mother 'Possum, or Skunky himself might have been passing right under where that tree fell."

"Oh no, I don't think so," said Mrs. Raccoon. "That is, I don't think it would be Skunky. We would have smelled—" Oh, dear, she was certainly putting her paw in her mouth tonight. She shouldn't have referred to anyone's smell at a time like this. Besides, Skunky didn't smell bad most of the time. And if he

5

were smashed under the dead hickory, it would certainly leave a gap in their friendly community where everyone, although quite individualistic, wished everyone else well most of the time. "No one else is moving," she said. "Listen—how quiet it is."

It was true. A brooding stillness hung in the air. Frogs, jarflies, beetles, and bugs had all brought their various peepings and ploppings and raspings and racketings and dronings and drummings to an abrupt stop.

But the stillness had only served to soothe Mr. Raccoon. "Scared out of their wits, they are," he said, already half out the doorway.

"Then I'm coming too," said Mrs. Raccoon, thinking that her mate's bravery under such circumstances ought to make him eligible for the annual Deep Forest Award. Being somewhat faster than Mr. Raccoon, she backed into him before they reached the ground, causing them both to fall, and the night was suddenly loud with their thrashing around to get righted and braced for whatever might lay before them.

2
The Neighbours Investigate

Up at the far end of the Grassy Meadow, a little way back into the Deep Forest, Squirrel was only slightly awakened by the big noise. He turned over, went back to sleep, and dreamed that an acorn had dropped from a tree somewhere, an acorn so big it shook the ground and would have been enough food for him, all his children, and his children's children for years and years to come if he could preserve it and keep it a secret. But then he supposed an acorn that big couldn't be kept a secret. Anyway, it would be selfish not to share it with all his kind. His tail twitched with impatience at his ungenerous dream thought. He flipped over in his bed and dreamed another dream where he, being in a more charitable mood, had called out all the squirrel population to start digging a hole big enough to store the huge acorn. It was to be as big around as half the Grassy Meadow and as deep as the pine tree that grew in the centre of the Deep Forest.

Old Owl, sitting in that very pine tree, had heard the noise. A quick but quite quakish quiver passed over his body, leaving several feathers out of place. He murmured a low "Whoooo?" and let it go at that, because, try as he might, when scared he had never been able to put a whole sentence together such as "Who goes there?" or "Who made that loud noise?" which would have been pretty pertinent questions right now. It would be some little time before he would feel himself again.

Mother 'Possum heard the great Crack-Splat-Slam-Whomp! and went to poke her nose out the end of her hollow log home to have a look around. The sudden vibration had shook her youngsters loose from her back, where they liked to cling until they got a little more used to the world. Seeing nothing unfamiliar, she settled down to see if anything or anyone might come by to give her a piece of news. It was good to breathe the fresh air after being cooped up in the one long, log room with seven children clambering over her back all the time. She really needed a larger log, one with turning-around room. Come morning, she just might load up the kids and strike out to see if that big noise may have created some interesting possibilities.

Skunky, not at all under where the dead tree lay, as Mr. Raccoon had direfully proposed, had been strolling through the Grassy Meadow on his way home from a night prowl and saw the whole thing, which delighted him enormously, for if there was one thing Skunky liked to do, it was report the local news. If no one else had witnessed an event, he liked also to add suitable flourishes here and there to bring as much drama as he could into the lives of his friends. Being a good reporter helped to bolster his own ego, for he knew there were times when, for his self-protection, he had been forced to make things quite smelly in the community.

As it turned out, Skunky actually was the only one to see the dead hickory fall, but he was not the first one to arrive at the place of the falling, for he had paused several times while crossing the Grassy Meadow to rehearse how he was going to tell the story to his friends in case they hadn't seen it, or maybe even in case they had. Everyone saw things from different angles, and who was to say what angle he saw it from? "Yes, I was the first to arrive at the scene," he would say with a good deal of importance. "In fact, I was there when it happened, you might say. Had to jump sixteen feet, ten inches to get out of the way."

But when Skunky arrived, he could plainly see there were too many witnesses for him to add that little fanciful folderol. Mr. and Mrs. Raccoon had already crawled all over the trunk and branches of the prone tree, peered, pawed, sniffed, and snuffed into holes to see if any of their friends of the Grassy Meadow, Deep Forest, or Rustling Brook were hurt or in need of help. They were now sitting on the topmost branch of the fallen tree in order to see as far as they could into such matters as the coming of a foe.

Rabbit had hopped from his home in the plum thicket to see what the commotion was. Being not at all good at climbing, he sat a few feet away and watched to see what the raccoons might discover, ready to offer what help he could. Several frogs had hopped over from the Rustling Brook and sat in a straight row, winking and blinking.

"It knocked us out of bed," said Mrs. Raccoon, noticing Skunky's arrival.

"I thought something had fallen from the sky," added Rabbit.

"Collapsed at last, did it?" commented Skunky, which was not at all the way he had planned to start talking about this event.

Head Frog and the lesser frogs just winked and blinked, being still speechless with fear.

Mother 'Possum, carrying her brood of children on her back and thus waddling around considerably,

9

was the last to arrive at the scene of the big noise before it became good daylight. "Is anyone hurt?" she asked.

"We can't find anyone," Mrs. Raccoon replied. "Mr. Raccoon said the woodpeckers left last week. They were living there, you know. Of course, someone may be under the tree."

Mother 'Possum, thinking to stake out a claim to a newer and maybe fresher smelling home if no one else had put in a bid, shuffled around to inspect the trunk where it had snapped loose from the roots to see if there might be a suitable hollow place.

"Now, what we'll have to do," planned Mr. Raccoon," is to send word around for everyone we know to meet here, and we'll take a census to see if anyone is missing."

"I'll do it," volunteered Skunky, thinking of the many times he'd get to tell the interesting story.

"I'll be faster," Rabbit said, seeing at last where he could be of some help.

Mrs. Raccoon's brow furrowed with deep thinking. "But if we notify everyone we know to come, won't that be a sort of census in itself?"

"You're right," Mr. Raccoon admitted, giving Mrs. Raccoon a nod of appreciation for straightening his thinking, which, if he said so himself, was often so muddled. "Well then, let's form a Search and Recovery Committee and get it done quickly. Skunky, you take the Deep Forest, clear over to the Shining River. Check on Beaver and Muskrat. Rabbit, you take the Grassy Meadow. Don't miss a mouse. Frogs, you take the Brook. I'll go over to the wheat field, right up to the farmer's barn."

"Better let me do that," suggested Rabbit. "I can get away faster in case Dog awakes."

"All right, Rabbit, you take the wheat field and I'll take the meadow."

"Listen!" Mrs. Raccoon demanded, holding up a silencing paw. "I heard something!"

"Dog?" asked Mr. Raccoon, Mother 'Possum, Rabbit, and Skunky, all at the same time.

"No, it was more like a 'cheep, cheep'."

"Where from?" asked Mother 'Possum.

"Right around here somewhere," replied Mrs. Raccoon. She walked over to where a limb of the fallen hickory had lodged in a multiflora rosebush that grew in the hedgerow.

They all looked and looked, even the frogs, although they were terribly nearsighted when out of water.

Rabbit raised his ears as high as they could go and twisted them forward and sideways, but all he heard was blue jays making a big fuss over Squirrel who was approaching the scene by way of the treetops.

"There it is again!" Mrs. Raccoon exclaimed.

"Yes, I distinctly heard it too," said Skunky. "It's on the ground somewhere."

At this the frogs began hopping around briskly. Being closer to the ground, they thought they might be the first to find whatever was going, "Cheep, cheep."

"It sounds something like a little chicken," said Mother 'Possum.

"Ain't no chickens around here," Mr. Raccoon said, giving Skunky and Mrs. Raccoon a sly look. He did not need to add that a mother hen from the neighbouring farm had once tried to secretly hatch her chickens in the plum thicket and met with such discouragement from the local residents that neither she nor any of her kind ever tried again.

"Here it is!" cried Head Frog, for he had hopped

11

right on top of a damp, lumpy looking thing—the very thing which earlier had made the Thud-Gasp sound that no one heard but which now went, "Cheep, cheep," in a most despairing way.

"Oh, Head Frog, hop off. It's a little bird," Mrs. Raccoon said.

Head Frog hopped off immediately. He'd been stepped on once himself and nearly squashed into a green greasy spot.

"Oh, I beg your pardon," he said to the lumpy looking thing. He winked and blinked but couldn't make out a thing that looked like a bird.

"I thought you said the woodpeckers left." Mrs. Raccoon turned questioningly to her mate.

"They did. I saw them. There's more birds around here than just woodpeckers. It could be a thrush, a sparrow, a warbler, a vireo, a wagtail, a pipit, a swallow. Goodness, we have lots of birds in these parts." Mr. Raccoon looked properly knowledgeable of the local feathered citizens.

"There's a heap too many blue jays," said Squirrel, coming headfirst down a tree to join the group on the ground. "Quarrel, quarrel, quarrel. That's all they ever do when I'm moving through the woods just minding my own business, enjoying the morning. What made the big noise last night? Oh, I say, it must have been the old hickory. Fell down at last, did it? Well, high time. Been standing there many a year. I remember my great-great-great-great-great-grandmother telling about nuts from that old tree."

"Well, this bird, whatever it is, needs help and quick," said Mrs. Raccoon, ignoring Squirrel's chatter. She turned it over so that it was right side up. "Its eyes are closed," she announced glumly.

Head Frog shaded his eyes with a front foot, for the morning sunlight was growing stronger. He could see that the lump had a head and beak and some little projections that looked like wings and maybe a tail. "Is it breathing?" he inquired.

Mrs. Raccoon leaned closer. "It sure doesn't seem to be." She poked it gently, but now not even a faint "Cheep, cheep" came forth.

Head Frog swelled with much importance, as head frogs sometimes do, and said, "Does anyone around here know about mouth to mouth resuscitation?"

"Resusci what?" asked Mr. Raccoon and Skunky and Rabbit and Squirrel, properly impressed by such a word.

Head Frog swelled a little more. "Well, I've seen a lot in my time, living around water as I do, and one thing I've learned about is resuscitation. R-E-S-U-S-C-I-T-A-T-I-O-N," he spelled. "Although there are several ways, the best way seems to be mouth to mouth." He looked around at the congregation to make sure he had their full attention. It wasn't often he could make a

13

speech. "The victim does not need to be put into any certain position. It can even be done when it is all crumpled up or half out of water. At least the half where the mouth is. And it can be little or big. No equipment needed but a good pair of lungs. The way you do it is merely open the victim's mouth, pull the chin up, take a deep breath, place your mouth over the victim's mouth, hold its nose, and blow your breath into its mouth until you see its chest rise."

"Yes, yes, Head Frog. What next? Hurry, get to the point," pleaded Mrs. Raccoon.

"Well, then you take your mouth away and watch the chest closely to see if the air you blew in comes out. It's called exhalation, or breathing out. As soon as you see this, do the whole thing over again and again and again and again, until you see the victim breathing on his own."

"Head Frog, if that is what is needed now, get to it," ordered Mrs. Raccoon. Having put her mind to it, she was quite bent on saving this little bird's life. And, as always, in circumstances like these she spoke to the Keeper of All Creatures, asking for His unfailing help in time of trouble. Sometimes she could get her words in order. Other times, in the hurry and worry of the moment, they came out brokenly, just a word here and there. Sometimes there were only sobs, but she knew the Keeper heard. Right now all she said was, "Oh, Great Keeper, here's a little one in need."

Head Frog hopped closer to the bird and was very much embarrassed after such an important explanatory speech to have to ask if the bird had a nose.

"Just open his beak and put the whole thing in your mouth and I think you'll get the nose too," Mrs. Raccoon said.

Head Frog did as commanded.

Such a commotion followed his first effort that he

14

hopped backward a great distance to be out of the way. The little bird's eyes flew open. It "Cheep, cheep, cheeped" madly and scrabbled about first this way, then that, making a rickety figure eight, a figure four, a figure six, and a little *i*, pecking a dot over it.

The baby 'possums were so scared their feet curled up tightly, pulling the hair on Mother 'Possum's back. She yelled, "Ouch" and jumped sideways, upsetting Mr. Raccoon, who wasn't used to being knocked over by an opossum and came up muttering darkly, even though he knew it was an accident. Squirrel hurriedly hopped up on the fallen tree for a better view of the whole turbulence. Rabbit crouched low on the ground as if to make himself invisible. Skunky automatically turned his back and raised his tail in readiness for his own type of protection.

"No, no, Skunky," Mrs. Raccoon screamed, fearing Skunky was going to spray them all with his obnoxious perfume.

"Well," Skunky said, a little shame-faced. "A body has instinctive impulses, you know."

"Of course, Skunky. We understand," said Mrs. Raccoon. "But there's no danger here. This little old bird can't hurt anything. It's just scared to death and, in my opinion, has a broken wing. A limb of the fallen tree must have hit it or maybe knocked it out of a nest somewhere."

At this, Mr. Raccoon, Rabbit, Squirrel, Head Frog and the lesser frogs, Mother 'Possum and babies all crept cautiously back and formed a circle to inspect the bird that had so suddenly come to life and caused such a stir.

"Is it a blue jay?" asked Squirrel. There was not much sorrow reflected in his voice.

"No," said Mr. Raccoon. "Beats me, though, what it is. Not red. Not blue. Not purple. Not brown. Not black. Just brownish black with polka-dots on its underneath side."

"Well, I've seen little birds grow up to be big birds that didn't look at all when they were big birds like they did when they were little birds," chattered Squirrel.

"That's right," said Mrs. Raccoon. "I wonder where the mother is or if there are any more little ones?" She looked worriedly at the area around the fallen tree.

Mother 'Possum circled the hickory stump again. Squirrel bounded farther up the tree trunk where he could get a wider view of the ground. Skunky ranged out into the Grassy Meadow. Mr. Raccoon poked at broken branches, twigs, and pieces of bark that had been scattered by the fall of the great hickory which had brought much of the undergrowth of the hedgerow down with it. Mrs. Raccoon stayed close to the small bird, saying soothing things like, "There, there, birdie. You'll be all right. We'll take care of you. You're among friends, and there is nothing better in the whole world than a good friend."

When the searchers could find no creature, living or dead, nearby, nor any tails, feet, head, beaks, or fur sticking from under the hickory tree, they held another brief meeting, resolved to inquire of all the local bird families whether a child was missing, and then bounded, hopped, walked, and waddled toward their appointed places in search of their other friends—all except Mrs. Raccoon who stayed by the "cheeping" bird.

3

Mrs. Raccoon Takes Charge of Little Mocker

The little bird cocked its head first one way, then the other, trying with his young and inexperienced brain to make out what this big furry creature was that talked so comfortingly. To all such questions such as "Where's your mother? Any brothers or sisters? What kind of a bird are you? Does your wing hurt much?" he could only respond, "Cheep, cheep, cheep," for he was too scared and his throat too tight to speak in the universal language of meadow, woods, and streams. Had it not been so, he might have answered, "I am a mockingbird. I have a brother and sister called Songer and Melody and a mother and father who named me Little Mocker, but I don't know where they are, nor where I am. Yesterday I flew and flew and flew, miles and miles and miles. I got so tired when nighttime came I went to bed, up there in that bush. Next thing I knew, something went 'Crack-Splat-Slam-Whomp.' It knocked me out of the bush and hit my wing and it hurts dreadfully and I am out of breath and scared and lonely and a while ago something green tried to eat me alive, head first. Oh, cheep, cheep, cheep."

A splinter of pain thrust itself down Little Mocker's wing and along his back. Tears fell from his eyes and mingled with the dew diamonds of the Grassy Meadow. He closed his eyes again, thinking all the horrible nightmares and the pain would go away and he would in some miraculous way be back in the nest with his mother hovering nearby, ready with his breakfast. But instead he sensed something even worse to be happening. A shadow hovered over him, shutting out the warmth of the morning sun. His eyes flew open just in time to see a pink cavernous mouth stretch open wide, and feel it close again at the back of his neck. So the big furry creature who had seemed friendly was going to eat him! He scrabbled and squawked with mingled pain and panic, fluttered his good wing, twitched his stubby tail feathers, and scratched with his feet at whatever part of the furry creature he could reach until he was quite out of breath again and knew instinctively that he must stop his hysterics or his body would be drained of its dwindling energy and his brain would cease to function entirely. In that case he might very well be eaten alive and never see the wide, beautiful, musical world he had thought so wonderful until the great Crack-Splat-Slam-Whomp!

Little Mocker went limp, letting his head and wings and feet and tail flop, flip, and flap whichever way they would, which was just about every way, for he was swinging, swaying, and swiveling about in the air, being held by only a tuft of tiny neck feathers. He soon realized that the furry creature was not eating him, but carrying him along somewhere in its mouth, and with a great deal of tenderness at that, for it could have taken him by the head or tail or injured wing and let him bump along on rocks and rails and briars and stinging weeds. As it was, his whole body, including his dangling feet, were kept well above these obstacles.

When they came to a big tree, instead of going around it as Little Mocker had expected, his carrier started straight up the trunk, crawled through a round hole, and deposited him on something which he was later to know as Mrs. Raccoon's beautiful Flower Garden quilt. How wonderfully soft it felt, almost like the home nest he had so recently abandoned. He let out a small sigh, a faint "cheep, cheep," and lay still, but with eyes wide open to see what would come next.

"Now then," said Mrs. Raccoon, "we will have to do something about your wing. Mr. Raccoon and the others may be gone for half a day, and the sooner we set the broken wing, the better." She began looking around for things with which to work. She would need a short, strong stick and some kind of binding material to tie the stick to the wing so that it would be held rigid until it healed. "It will take no time at all to heal in one so young," Mrs. Raccoon continued in a most reassuring way. "Mr. Raccoon was much older than you when I set his leg. Got it broken in a fight with a dog, he did, but outfought that hound tooth and nail, and made it home all right. And if you'll notice, he doesn't limp at all. My goodness, this house is in a mess, but first things first." She turned a corner of the quilt over the little bird so that it would absorb the wetness of the morning dew through which it had floundered.

Finding no stick of suitable length and strength in her home, Mrs. Raccoon decided she must go outside again to look for one. She was halfway down her home tree when the thought struck her that the injured bird might get worried and scared and flabbergasted while she was gone and flutter, flip, and fall right out the doorway, breaking the other wing, or leg, foot, toe, beak, whatever there was about a bird to break. Really, she was quite inexperienced in raising birds, but would accept the task, of course, and count it a pleasure since she had no little ones of her own this spring.

She scurried back up, and saw that her patient was

still wrapped in the quilt. Nevertheless, as she backed out the doorway, she pulled the little tin bucket behind her to block the passage. Then she made straightway for the hedgerow where the hickory had fallen. In a very short time she found a straight stout stick to her liking. She laid it aside and looked around for something with which to tie the stick to the wing. It must be strong yet soft so as not to cut into the flesh, such flesh as a bird's wing had. Looked all just bones and feathers to her; yet she remembered there had been a spot or two of blood, so there must be flesh. She inspected the tendrils on some wild grapevines and stems of the Grassy Meadow millet, but at length decided that she must go all the way to the dump pile to get something soft and workable. There were lots of old rags and tags and bits and bobs at the dump pile.

Mrs. Raccoon really disliked going to the dump pile in daylight because so often People came while she was there and threw out boxes of things they didn't want, and other People came and went through these boxes of thrown-out things to see if there was anything they did want, and no matter how stealthily she tried to get away, almost always someone would shout, "Look, there's a raccoon!" Just as if she were some kind of freak with two tails or six noses. They never said anything complimentary like, "Look, that one has seven rings around its tail," or "How precise and in place is her black mask!" And they must think her coat beautiful, else why would they make coats for themselves of raccoon fur, and caps, and tail banners to hang from bicycle bars? The idea of being made into a cap made her shudder and although in a hurry, she purposely stopped to look around and get her thoughts started in another more pleasant direction. She was a firm believer that this could be done and often prescribed this for her friends who sometimes got themselves into a frenzied state just thinking of what might happen and which mostly never did.

She was deliberately considering the crowsfoot violets, how the two top petals were a darker colour than the three bottom ones, when a slight movement to her right, in a hole at the base of an old stump, caught her attention. In fact, it was two movements, shiny and round, that blinked off and on like twin fireflies, only not so bright. They were eyes, of course, but whose? She shaded her own to see if she could bring a face for the eyes into focus.

"That you, Chuck?" she inquired, for the conspicuous pile of dirt at the entrance to the hole was a telltale sign of a woodchuck home. But then it could be a weasel or fox or any number of other animals that took over woodchuck homes from time to time.

"Guess?" came a tiny, muffled voice from inside, obviously meant to be disguised and indicating readiness for an hour or two of play this bright and dazzling morning.

"I have no time for games, whoever you are," said Mrs. Raccoon. "I'm on my way, fast, to the dump pile for a string of sorts because the big hickory fell down and I've a bird to mend and adopt, I suspect, and since you're not squashed under the tree you can help us hunt for our friends."

"Whatever on earth are you saying?" asked Chuck, emerging from his den in a hurry with several wrinkles in his brow. Poor Mrs. Raccoon must have a fever and be quite out of her mind. "Could I get you a drink of water? Won't you come in and lie down a while?" It was plain to Chuck that Mrs. Raccoon had something serious on her mind and, in Chuck's opinion, one could drop dead having to grapple with serious things in the morning.

"Oh, water barter, and lie down bye down! There's been a catastrophe, Chuck. Come along, and I'll straighten it out for you, and you can help me hunt for a string. And let's hurry!"

"Well, you didn't look to be in a hurry staring at those violets in my front yard that way," said Chuck.

"It was just for a moment while I was trying to get my mind off having my fur made into a cap," Mrs. Raccoon explained. But she could see from Chuck's expression that she was only complicating things, so as they hurried along she began at the beginning with the great Crack-Splat-Slam-Whomp! and brought Chuck up to date, with only small interruptions from Chuck such as, "Was that what the noise was?" and "Oh my! Too bad," and "Tut, tut."

By this time they were at the dump pile, and to Mrs. Raccoon's pleasure, there was no one else there.

Old bottomless buckets, pans, bottles, furnace filters, coffee cans, beer cans, broken chairs, punched-out screen doors, headless dolls, cracked flower pots, kitchen sinks, automobile tyres, and lots of other peculiar and unrecognizable things were turned over and pawed aside.

Chuck called out from time to time, asking if

some rubber bands, an old typewriter ribbon, a piece of fishing line, or some florist wire would do, but Mrs. Raccoon said they must keep looking for something softer. "You see, when I wrap it around the hickory stick, I'll have to go in between the wing feathers, which look to be as though they grow mighty close together."

Chuck admitted that he didn't know much about wing feathers, but good-naturedly kept on looking. "If we'd run in to D.P. (which is what everyone called Dump Pile Rat), he could probably find, right away, what you're looking for," he told Mrs. Raccoon.

The sun rose higher, the breezes got warmer, and traffic thickened along the road running beside the dump pile. So intense was their search for just the right thing that neither Mrs. Raccoon nor Chuck noticed that a truck had backed up to the edge of the dump pile and that a Man and Boy were preparing to lift the tailgate and send down another load of old papers, shoes, broken lamps, oil cans, chicken coops, coal cinders, crepe paper flowers, and no telling what else.

In the few seconds before the avalanche began, Mrs. Raccoon shouted to Chuck, "I have it. This is just the thing." Chuck rushed over to her side to see what it was, and a voice up above shouted, "Dad, there's a raccoon. Just what I've been looking for."

The rubbish had already begun to cascade. Chuck was hit first by an old umbrella, and Mrs. Raccoon suffered the blow of a plastic egg carton. In no time at all they were covered by all the other items of rubbish.

Mrs. Raccoon, already having had such an alarming morning, began to shake, which made the bottles and cans and bottomless buckets all around them clatter and clang and rattle and give out very strong clues as to where they were.

Chuck, who was quite used to living underground

and tunneling himself in and out of places, was not at all alarmed, and after having determined that neither of them was seriously injured, tried to comfort his companion. "Don't worry," he whispered. "We'll get out of here. There's plenty of air and look, here is a peephole of sunlight. We'll go in that direction and make a dash for the woods when we get out."

"Not yet, Chuck. Not yet," moaned Mrs. Raccoon. "My legs are too weak. I couldn't run. Let us remain hidden. Didn't you hear what that Boy said? I just know he wants my tail or my whole coat. If he has a stick that barks fire, he could kill either one of us or both before we made it to the woods."

Chuck was too respectful and compassionate to say that as long as Mrs. Raccoon continued to quiver and shake and cause such a rattle, they weren't at all hidden. Any moment, a hand could be thrust down through the rubbish and catch them by an ear or a leg or a tail, whatever was handy. Already he heard footsteps up above crashing in their direction. The ominous sound made Chuck think faster than he ever had in his whole life. Having been used to doing his thinking leisurely while basking in the sun on some grassy bank, he later marveled at the speed with which the thoughts marched through his mind, in proper order, full of logic and quickly conclusive. *One: The Boy said he wanted a raccoon. Two: My own fur, in the eyes of Man, is cheap. Three: I have never seen a woodchuck tail hanging from bicycle bars, nor a woodchuck cap. Four: Mrs. Raccoon is my friend, a good and kindly neighbour. Five: I can get to the surface of the dump quicker than she. Six: Once there, I will pause long enough to be seen, then dive back in.*

With no doubt or hesitation whatever, he rattled off his plan to Mrs. Raccoon and, not waiting for comment, plunged toward the peephole of light.

It worked even better than Chuck had planned.

24

When he paused on top of the dump so as to be plainly seen, he heard the Man say, "Boy, don't you know a woodchuck from a raccoon? Come on, let's go."

When the motor of the truck died away in the distance, Mrs. Raccoon began to make her way out of her hiding place. It was a noisy business. Things shifted and slid and banged against each other. At one place she stepped on a gaily painted boxlike contraption with fancy brass trimmed corners. She tried to pick off one of the shiny ornaments to take home and put on the shelf along with their other treasures. Suddenly some coloured lights inside the box began to wink and blink, and what sounded like a jumble of words came from a little hole in one side. It was like nothing she had ever seen, almost scary, yet so utterly desirable with all its shiny trimmings. However, she couldn't get anything loose from it, and the whole thing was much too big for her to carry. So, clutching the half-used ball of purple wool, which was what she had found and decided would be just the thing for the wing-setting, she made her noisy way to the surface.

Chuck was already out of the dump pile and waiting when Mrs. Raccoon emerged. He started to accompany her back home, but Mrs. Raccoon, berating herself for lingering so long when there was a patient to attend, moved along so fast that Chuck decided it would be better for him to go off at his own pace and look for other friends and neighbours, or stop and rest his muscles and head, especially his head after all that unusual thinking so early in the morning.

4

"Come Back, Little Mocker"

When Mrs. Raccoon blocked the doorway and departed for the dump pile, Little Mocker, who had already had such a bad day's beginning, began to imagine all sorts of terrible things that might still happen. Maybe the furry creature who had brought him here just wasn't hungry now and was saving him for lunch or supper. Little jagged points of fear, which somehow had been momentarily lulled away by the warm comfort of the quilt, returned and danced a fast jig up and down his spine. Perhaps he wouldn't ever again see the sun or feel the warm breezes ruffle his feathers or loop through the air with gay abandon or hear his mother's approving voice. Just yesterday she had said, "You do fly well, Little Mocker. Tomorrow we will have our first singing lesson."

It was the thought of missing this first singing lesson that brought Little Mocker's mind away from the brink of panic and dark despair. He did so want to be a good singer. Maybe he could be the best in the whole world! He would rise high in the air, spilling silvery notes from his throat, and come down in a sparkly cascade of song that would make all the other birds gather round and say such things as "How do you do it, Little Mocker? Never have we heard such wild and beautiful music." But first he must get back home, and to get back home he must see if he could fly with one wing. It was a long, long way he had come, and he wasn't sure of his way back. What must his mother and father and sister and brother be thinking? Perhaps it would have been better if he hadn't learned to fly so quickly and so well.

He flipped back the cover and fluttered about the circular room, cringing with pain. In the semidarkness created by the bucket blocking the entranceway, he bumped his head on a shelf and hurt his foot on some splintery glass. The broken wing dragged along, of no use at all. He looked at it curiously, wondering why it failed to respond to his desire to fly and why it hurt so much.

Although there was very little space in this room, he thought that by getting as close to the wall as he could, he might be able to see if he could get airborne before bumping into the opposite wall. Certainly he couldn't go upward, for he had observed that there was a wall at the top too. Such a peculiar room. Not at all open and breezy as he was accustomed to. Pressing his tail against the wall, he flapped the good wing with all his might, but an odd thing happened. He went around in a circle and ended up with his beak against the wall from which he had started, with his tail sticking out into the room. He tried it again and again, but always with the same results. When he saw that it was of no use, he went back to the quilt in anguish of heart. Somewhere deep down inside of him he felt a sob gathering. Soon it reached the surface and was followed by another and another of greater intensity until every feather of his bedraggled plumage seemed to be shaking with grief. "Oh, this is the end of everything," he cried. "Never no more will I fly from lilac to wild rose, up and up into the green trees and down to the brook. Never no more stroll in the buttercups, pause in the brambles, and flutter among the wild sweet Williams. Never, never sing. Oh, never, never make the beautiful music." Waves of sorrow for what might have been swept over him, preventing further words. He cried and cried and cried, freely and helplessly and inconsolably.

After a while the cozy warmth of the quilt began to work its comforting magic. It seemed to puff in all the right places, holding the broken wing up so that it didn't hurt so and supporting the weary little head. The uncontrollable sobs grew farther and farther apart, and deep down where they had started came another feeling to replace them—one of sleepy lassitude and dim memory that the furry creature had said something about being able to mend the wing. Why take the trouble to mend a wing if the intention was to later make a meal of the whole body? A warm ray of hope suffused Little Mocker's body, and soon he was fast asleep.

When Mrs. Raccoon returned with hickory stick and ball of wool, she looked at the sleeping bird and decided not to start her bone-setting activities until the little fellow woke up. "A good sleep after such an ordeal will do him good," she said to herself and set about straightening the house.

First she dusted the scallop-edged shelf, then picked up the shiny treasures and put them back in place, being sure to put the blue Vicks Vapo-rub jar where the sun, streaming in through the open doorway, would touch it around two o'clock and light up the whole room with a lovely colour. All the while she sang, softly, a little made-up tune of thanks.

> Troubles come and troubles go
> When Keeper's blessings to us flow.
> Thank you, Keeper of us all,
> We who tremble, faint, and fall.

When everything was in order, she went to the doorway to see if anyone had returned with a report from the neighbours. Her thoughts turned to Chuck and how he had managed to get them both safely out of the dump pile this morning. It was things like that which made one deserving of the Deep Forest Award.

When Little Mocker awakened, he wondered for a moment where he was. He looked around for the familiar lilac bush where the home nest had been. Then, with a flurry of his heart, he remembered everything. He blinked his eyes and cocked his head to one side. The little room to which he had been carried seemed a bit more friendly with strong daylight coming in the opened doorway. The broken wing, lulled into comfort by rest and sleep, did not hurt at all. With a great leap of his tiny heart, he thought that it was healed and all he had to do was hop over to the doorway and fly off triumphantly into the jolly, warm, waiting world outside. He saw the furry creature picking up seeds and putting them into a tin bucket and wondered if he should say something and if so, what. Maybe he should thank it for picking him up out of harm's way and bringing him here for a healing nap, but in all honesty he preferred the great free outdoors, and if no one minded he'd be on his way. Or perhaps he ought to just take off while the furry creature wasn't noticing.

A little breeze wafted in through the open doorway, bringing the smell of honeysuckle and wild sweet William and behind that the faint odour of a newly ploughed field. It was like an invisible little hand beckoning and tugging him homeward. The more he thought of being out there right now, flitting from sassafras tree to plum thicket to elderberry, the more he wanted to just escape without further delay of any sort. The distant ringing call of a meadowlark and the nearer trill of a field sparrow reinforced this desire so overwhelmingly that he raised up on his feet and attempted to take off toward the doorway, But, alas, once again he was going around in circles, and a stabbing pain shot from his shoulder clear down to his toenails. The broken wing wasn't healed after all.

To cover his disappointment, confusion, pain, and the bad manners of attempting to go off without so much as a good-bye and thank you, he tried to act as if he were only making himself more comfortable in the quilt.

He looked at the furry creature who was now staring at him with sharp but friendly eyes. "My name is Little Mocker," he said in a voice that he hoped would sound dignified and mannerly, but which in truth came out all trembly and high-pitched.

"Oh, so you're a mockingbird," said Mrs. Raccoon as if quite pleased with this fact. "Well, I am Mrs. Raccoon. I was beginning to think you weren't old enough to talk. We couldn't tell from your markings and colour what kind of bird you were."

"When I'm a little older I'll have white stripes down my tail and across my wings like Mother."

"Where is your mother?"

"I don't know," replied Little Mocker and set about telling of his faraway home and family, who he would have told about earlier if he hadn't been so scared, winding up with the announcement that he would like to fly back home immediately for the singing lesson that would start today.

"We will have to set the broken wing first, and then it will take a while for it to heal," Mrs. Raccoon said. "But you will be able to fly again," she added quickly, observing the look of fear and disappointment on Little Mocker's face.

There was a moment of silence after which Little Mocker inquired in a small voice, "What do you do to set a wing?"

At this, Mrs. Raccoon showed Little Mocker the hickory stick and the wool and described how she would place the stick along the broken wing and bind it with the wool so the bone ends would stay opposite each other and grow back together.

"I suppose it will hurt," Little Mocker said.

"Only a little at first," Mrs. Raccoon assured. "And much less if you will let me have your cooperation."

"What is cooperation?" Little Mocker wanted to know, stumbling a bit over the word and slightly alarmed.

"In this case it is being still and not moving your wing or flopping around while I am working on it."

Another waft of sweet spring air reached Little Mocker's nose as if it had been blown in at the proper time to administer a reminder that the whole wonderful world was still out there, waiting, and missed him and wanted him back, so there would be no missing parts. Indeed, it seemed as if the little breezes blowing across the meadow grasses, bending blade against blade like bows across strings, manufactured little musical words that made their way into the hole in the white oak and whispered just to him, "Come back, Little Mocker. Get your wing fixed and come back. Come back. Come back."

"I will. I will," said Little Mocker in a sweet ecstasy of response to the call of the meadow. When he saw that Mrs. Raccoon was moving purposefully close with stick and string, he realized she had thought he was speaking to her. For a moment there was a puzzlement in his breast. Would it be honest to let her think that? Would it be right to take his answer away from the breezes and give it to Mrs. Raccoon? Would the breezes cease to speak to him? With a small sigh he thought there must be many fine points to honesty. It would take more living to have quick answers. For the time being, he felt a necessary corrective would be to give Mrs. Raccoon an answer of her own. So, for her, he repeated, "I will. I will."

While she worked, Mrs. Raccoon kept up a steady stream of talk, telling Little Mocker how Mr. Raccoon and Squirrel and Mother 'Possum and Rabbit and all the frogs and Chuck had gone to check on other friends and neighbours to see if everything was all right with them. "If we find them all, then we'll know no one is under the fallen tree." Because she had a thumb and fingers that made her deft with strings and small things, she placed the stick and wound the yarn with expertise.

Even before Mrs. Raccoon had tied the last knot, Little Mocker knew that he was experiencing less pain. But even better than the cessation of pain was the knowledge that he was in a community where folks cared what happened to each other. It gave him such a good feeling. "I wish that I could go too," he said.

"Oh, there are plenty of lookers," Mrs. Raccoon assured. "We will soon know. Now let us have some breakfast. I have some millet seed, sunflower seed, rose-hips, and corn."

Little Mocker, being hungrier than he supposed, enjoyed the food. But gratitude welled up so enormously in him that with his mouth yet full of millet seed he blurted out, "I wish I could do something."

"Oh, you will, Little Mocker. You will. Someday you will make beautiful music for all of us. You may entertain at our summer picnics and autumn banquets."

Mrs. Raccoon spoke with such assurance that Little Mocker was comforted. After the remains of breakfast had been cleared away, he worked himself in a zigzag fashion back to the quilt and nestled in its downy warmth.

5
No
One
Missing

By midafternoon the searchers and reporters began to trickle back to the fallen hickory. Mrs. Raccoon, feeling that Little Mocker was calm and steady enough not to fall out, helped him to a vantage point near the doorway where he could see all that went on outside. She then descended to the ground and took a seat on top of the fallen tree trunk to watch for the incoming neighbours.

Rabbit, being fast and most eager to see if all was well, was the first to return. With sleek brown hair glistening in the sun and white stubby tail punctuating his leaps, he came bounding, big-eyed, along the hedgerow, bursting with the good news that all was well with the bobwhites, the field sparrows, the meadowlarks. "And the meadow mice are all accounted for," he said, not without a shade of pride for this accomplishment. "They'll be along later to learn of the outcome, but six of the meadow mice babies had the stomach ache and had to stay in bed a while. I would have been back even sooner, but most of them had scattered for the day and had to be found."

"How many are there now?" asked Mrs. Raccoon.

"Fifty-six!"

"My, my," said Mrs. Raccoon admiringly. "What a nice family."

"How is the little bird?" Rabbit inquired, looking around for the invalid.

Mrs. Raccoon pointed toward her doorway where Little Mocker was watching. "He's a mockingbird, Rabbit. I have set his broken wing, and all will be well." She raised her voice and called, "Little Mocker, this is Rabbit."

Little Mocker blinked his eyes and nodded politely.

Rabbit, looking at Little Mocker, flicked an ear in response.

"I haven't seen any mockingbirds in these parts for a long time," said Rabbit, continuing his conversation with Mrs. Raccoon.

"Nor I," replied Mrs. Raccoon. "Little Mocker has indicated that he came from far away."

Next to return was Squirrel. Then came Head Frog and the lesser frogs, Mr. Raccoon, and Mother 'Possum, all with good news that the ones they had been sent to find had been found, well and healthy. Many of the sought for had returned with the seekers, and others were coming later.

Skunky and his party were the last to arrive, for Skunky had taken time to tell of the fall of the great hickory with much detail.

Speaking to Chipmunk, he had said, "Yes, there she was, one minute a big, tall, dead hickory full of woodpecker holes, and the next minute, with no sign of wind or lightning or axe or ox, not even old Beaver, there she was, Crack-Splat-Slam-Whomp!, lying smashed up in the hedgerow. One of the Seven Modern Wonders, I shouldn't wonder." He stood up as tall as he could to indicate how the tree was before it fell, then fell down himself in an ungainly sprawl, seeing to it that his nose and legs and tail all pointed in opposite directions. He lay so still and quiet for such a long time that Chipmunk grew alarmed and began feeling for pulse and calling in soft and concerned tones, "Skunky, Skunky. Get you now, Skunky, up. Gone-dog-it!" Chipmunk, when excited, got his words all mixed up.

Skunky, enjoying it all, lay there as long as he could, then jumped up, laughing and slapping his thigh. Then he hurried off to check out the fox family, thinking up some new way of telling the tale all over again. As he walked along, he thought he might make a career of telling and retelling the story since he was the only one to see it fall. He would do little daily exercises, standing up and touching his hind toes with his front ones to keep agile and in good condition so he could make his sprawl in various and interesting ways. Maybe even after he was gone his friends would erect a little monument that would say:

Here lies Skunky who saw hickory fall
And made it dramatically known to all.

He walked along for some time, contemplating the epitaph on the little marker, until it made him nervous thinking of himself lying in the ground beneath it, unable to spin any more good yarns. He stopped, made a motion in the air with his paw as if to erase the whole thing, and began to practice how he would tell the foxes when he found them. "Yes, there she was, standing straight and tall just before good daylight, then suddenly, Crack-Splat-Slam-Whomp!"

By four o'clock everyone was accounted for and seated in a great circle at the edge of the Grassy Meadow. There was Muskrat and Beaver and Mink, Red Fox and Toad, two terrapins, fifty-six meadow mice, fourteen frogs, Chuck, Owl, Hawk, etc., etc. Many had brought picnic food, which they shared with all. They talked and talked, recounting the day's adventures. All inquired of the injured bird, and Mrs. Raccoon told how she had set the wing and would care for the little fellow until he was mended.

The stars came out, making a polka-dotted sky, and a big yellow moon climbed higher and higher. The little frogs played leapfrog, and the meadow mice organized a game of hopscotch.

If there were any lingering worries in the minds of the inhabitants of the Grassy Meadow, Deep Forest, and Rustling Brook that someone may have been smashed under the big hickory, possibly Little Mocker's mother who might have come looking for him, they were quickly dispelled the next day.

Before the sun had poked its long fingers between the trees of the Deep Forest, the high-pitched "zing" of a chain saw made the countryside tingle with sound. Little Mocker, waking from a night's sleep, demanded, "What is *that*?" Forgetting his injured wing, he instinctively braced himself for flight.

"They've come to cut up the dead tree and haul it

away," Mrs. Raccoon explained. She was watching from the doorway, but far enough back in the room so that if the sawyers should look up she would not be detected. Occasionally she saw a slight movement out in the Grassy Meadow or along the hedgerow which indicated to her that the neighbours were secretly gathering to watch the noisy proceedings. She knew that Mr. Raccoon was out there somewhere, too. He had gone out to gather something fresh for breakfast before the sawyers had come and now had to wait until they departed before he dared return.

By midmorning all trace of the dead tree was gone. The grass and shrubbery that had been bent over sprung back into shape. Squirrel, Skunky, Chuck, Mr. Raccoon, the frogs, and Mother 'Possum with her little 'possums came walking, hopping, waddling, riding, and jumping from different directions. Rabbit, who had been crouching behind a clump of burdock so long that his hind legs had gone to sleep, came wobbling into the circle in such a peculiar manner it set all the little frogs laughing, which they didn't often do, it being their custom to just wink and blink.

After inspecting the place where the tree had lain and finding not one single feather, hair, whisker, or fragment of skin, they all agreed that Little Mocker had been the only casualty. "And he is going to be all right," reported Mrs. Raccoon, coming into the circle of friends.

They all expressed their delight and a few, now that they were relieved, said that it had passed through their minds that another stranger to the community might have been wandering through and been caught under the tree.

"I suppose this Little Mocker's folks are worried about him, wherever they are," Mother 'Possum said. One of her own little 'possums had fallen off her back

39

on the way over this morning, and she had had to do some considerable zig-zagging back and forth across the meadow to find him again, a whimpering, dew-wet ball of pink-tailed misery.

"I thought about that all last night," Mrs. Raccoon confessed.

Everyone nodded to indicate that such a thought, if not lasting all night, had occurred to them too since the great fall.

"Well, what we'll have to do," said Mr. Raccoon in his best organizational voice, "is to make inquiries and send out reports far and near that we are in possession of a missing bird."

"Mercy, I haven't seen a mockingbird around these parts in years," said Skunky, who really wasn't but a year old himself.

There was a chorus of "Nor I's."

Mr. Raccoon looked toward the delegation of blue jays adorning the stump of the fallen tree, thinking perhaps they had ranged farther than some of the four-footed friends. "We don't know nothin'," they said very ungrammatically. And then one, a little bolder than the others, ventured the observation that birds of a feather flocked together, which was meant to indicate that they weren't brothers' keepers or anything like that for the mockingbirds.

Mr. Raccoon looked cross and said, "In this district we all flock together, whether we are feathered, furred, skinned, or scaled, and if there are any who do not wish to look after the welfare of others, I will personally escort them into the Next County."

"Yes sir, and I'll help," offered Squirrel, also scowling at the blue jays.

The blue jays hung their heads. And they shivered too. Everyone knew how bad off things were in the Next County where there was no organization, no brotherhood, just dog-eat-dog government and very bad behaviour.

The silence that followed was long and uncomfortable. Mr. Raccoon shuffled around nervously, trying to think how to soften his threat. Never ever would he really oust anyone into the Next County.

"What's the Next County?" asked the tiniest meadow mouse who hadn't lived long enough to know.

"It's a place where the inhabitants don't know how to live well and be happy. And I think it's because they don't know about the Keeper of All Creatures," explained Mrs. Raccoon.

"Oh, we's know about him, don't we?" said the tiniest mouse, looking around the circle, bright-eyed and baby-innocent.

All nodded in profound and silent agreement. Some bowed their heads. Others folded their paws across their chests. Mrs. Raccoon gave Mama Meadow Mouse an approving look. It must be hard to be as busy as she was with all her children and grandchildren and great-grandchildren and still see that they were taught first things first.

After a while Rabbit said that he was of a mind to go way down to the Big Piney this day, and he'd surely see lots of distant cousins and other acquaintances of whom he would inquire about missing birds.

Others, except Mother 'Possum who couldn't get away handily just now, said they too had planned trips later, sometime during the week.

"How long will it be before Little Mocker can fly again?" asked Rabbit. "Can he tell a person which way to start to look for his family?"

"It will be about two weeks if we can keep him still so the bones will knit," Mrs. Raccoon replied. "But even when his wing is mended, I don't know that he can find his way back from where he came. Sounds like a long, long way. He speaks of passing a waterfall and crossing a railroad track. Anyone know of such things?"

There was much scratching of head, furrowing of brows, and twisting of whiskers as the neighbours thought and thought. Finally Skunky voiced the opinion of all. "No such things in these parts."

6
Little Mocker's Recovery and Departure

Because he wished so much to get well, Little Mocker's recovery was speedy. Time did not drag. Mrs. Raccoon entertained him with so many pleasant stories about the local inhabitants, he came to feel that he had known them all a long time—Skunky, who liked to add a few little gewgaws to actual happenings; Rabbit, who always wanted to be helpful; Squirrel, who chattered so, no one paid much attention; Chipmunk, who sometimes tumbled his words out all mixed up; D.P. Rat, who lived in the enormous dump pile; Beaver, who was a fine fellow but didn't get away from the Shining River very often; Chuck; Mother 'Possum and the little 'possums; the blue jays; and the myriad of meadow mice.

One day while Mrs. Raccoon was thus describing the neighbours and at the same time serving a little midmorning snack of rosy-red rosehips, she said, more slowly than was her usual custom and with a soft, reverent quality in her voice Little Mocker had never heard before, "And, of course, there is the Keeper, in and out and 'roundabout amongst us all the time. Always ready to listen, to help, to pick us up and straighten us out when we make mistakes, if we want Him to. And He loves us all the time, whether we're lovable or not. A great friend, the Keeper." Her rich fur rippled as if from sweet ecstasy she could barely contain.

Little Mocker's heart was strangely warmed and stirred by these words. He pushed aside the rosehip he'd been pecking on and gave full attention. Mrs. Raccoon was looking directly at him, yet her eyes, sparkling like dew in morning sun, seemed focused somewhere through and beyond. He turned his head quickly to glance behind him. Seeing no one, he asked, "Have I seen the Keeper? I mean, was He there the morning I fell?" He wondered how he could have missed one of such greatness. He could tell by this special look in Mrs. Raccoon's eyes that this Keeper was by far the most important one in these parts.

"Yes. No. That is—I mean—yes, He was there, but, no, you didn't see Him. No one does. Except—" Her voice trailed off. She lifted a hand as if to go on, then let it fall again in a helpless gesture.

"Yes, yes. Except what?" Little Mocker urged, fearing Mrs. Raccoon was going to get caught up in some kind of dreamy trance just when he wanted to hear more.

"Well, except it does seem to me sometimes that I can see where He has just been." Mrs. Raccoon sighed wistfully.

"You mean like bent grass, or a footprint in the mud?" Little Mocker asked.

"Oh, no. Whenever I've seen something good or true or beautiful, it's as if He has just walked by. Yesterday, early, a shaft of sunshine, coming through the trees, looked so solid, it seemed as if one could climb right up to the sky on it. When I looked to where it pointed on the ground, I saw one of the meadow mice mired in a mud puddle. I mean mired! Clear up to his belly. Before I could get to it, Chuck walked by, snatched that mouse out, dangled him in the water 'til he was clean, and left him in the grass to dry. Now

44

there were plenty of footprints in the mud. Not the Keeper's, but—well, you see what I mean?"

Little Mocker nodded thoughtfully.

"He doesn't come in fur or feathers like you or me," Mrs. Raccoon continued. "You see, He is everywhere at once, ready to help, or talk to, or just to be still with. If He had a body that needed to walk or fly or swim, how could He get to some place, say way over in the Snowy Mountains or down in the Gloomy Swamp, miles and miles away, when He might be especially needed, and be up here in the Grassy Meadow at the same time, seeing that no one got smashed under the hickory tree?"

Little Mocker's heart beat faster and faster in a rapture of delight that there could be such a Great One, someone unseen but hovering over him right now, warm and protective, like his mother did back in the nest. Yet, there were some nagging questions pecking away at a corner of his mind.

"How do you know all this?" he asked straight out, hoping Mrs. Raccoon wouldn't think him brash or unmannered.

"It's been handed down. But even if it hadn't been, there are times you just know there is Someone greater than us, whether anyone has told you or not."

"But sometimes we do get smashed, all to bits," Little Mocker pursued, remembering a messy sight he'd seen on the railroad tracks, flying over.

"Oh, true, true," Mrs. Raccoon said sorrowfully. "But that's not because the Keeper isn't there. He lets us have our own way, and sometimes we make whopper-sized mistakes. But it is better to be free, risk the mistakes, and rely on His help than to be held by a chain or trap or cage and ordered to do this or that, or go here or there, or don't go here or there.'"

"He doesn't have a chain?" Little Mocker asked, more to keep the conversation going, for he feared Mrs. Raccoon was going to stop any moment.

"No. Yes. That is—" A wrinkle creased Mrs. Raccoon's brow. What must Little Mocker think with all these yes, no, that is answers she was coming up with. "Well," she began again, "His chain, if you can call it that, is unseen too. It doesn't wear any scuff marks around your neck or blisters on your ankles. If you feel it at all, it's maybe like a warm sunbeam."

"Oh, I think I'd like to feel it," Little Mocker interrupted eagerly.

"Well, it's like—it's like—" Mrs. Raccoon searched for words. "It's a warm feeling inside like you've come under His care and know it. We around here like to think of ourselves as being links in His chain rather than being held by it with no freedom. Goodness, when you're a link in the chain, you can still go anyplace, any time, anywhere." Mrs. Raccoon made all kinds of motions so as to show her freedom. She made a quick dart to the right, to the left, rolled up in a ball, turned a somersault, crawled up one wall of her room, across the ceiling, and down the other wall.

"Of course," she continued, somewhat out of breath, "once in a while some bad things of our own making get us by the tail and swing us around willy-nilly 'til we're no good to ourselves or anybody else. Most especially of no good to the Keeper, who uses us to do His good deeds. And sometimes bad things not of our making get hold of us too, just because they long ago slithered into the world and haven't been stomped out yet."

"Let's stomp 'em!" Little Mocker cried, having no idea of what to start stomping, but quite overcome with this new and wonderful knowledge of the ever-present Keeper and the audacity of anything to get between Him and His creatures. The mockingbird's eyes were flashing jet beads of determination, his body a fluffed-up ball of zeal, each individual feather a banner of quivering rage against bad things. He jumped up and down, toes spread apart, to demonstrate his ability to stomp, although with his skinny toes he was successful in raising only a few dust specks.

Mrs. Raccoon smiled. "Each must stomp in his own best way, Little Mocker, and maybe it won't be with our feet. But stomp we will!" She took Little Mocker by his one good wing, and they stomped symbolically all around the little room high in the white oak tree. The blue Vicks jar clitter-clattered against the little tin bucket. The Flower Garden quilt fluttered. A piece of wood fell from the ceiling. Mr. Raccoon, having climbed the tree and looked inside his home, stared in amazement and said, "Oh, my," and "Well, I'll be," and "What in the world!" and "Jimminyfaddledisticks!" He went back down and sat in the shade of the hickory

47

stump to give whatever flamdoodle was going on time to get over.

From time to time thereafter the neighbours came to visit Little Mocker. Those who could, climbed or flew to a branch near the raccoon doorway where they could carry on an easy conversation. Others who had to stay on the ground raised their voices—not only when they were talking to Little Mocker, but also when they were talking among themselves, so he wouldn't feel left out of things.

Little Mocker wasn't sure he'd be able to tell toads and frogs apart when later he might come upon them at closer range. But as Mrs. Raccoon said, there would be no harm in simply asking which one they were.

"Don't ever be afraid to ask a question," Mrs. Raccoon had said more than once during Little Mocker's convalescence. It was this advice that led him to ask his visitors what they meant if they used a big word he wasn't familiar with, or where was this Shining River and Big Piney they spoke of? And what was Dog and barking stick and fire and storm and picnics?

Even when he didn't ask, they'd explain about such things as Indian summer days when the woods and meadows were covered with a gauzy blue veil and smelled of wood smoke, hickory nuts, and crushed acorns, and how the hedgerow went absolutely mad with cricket song and seemed to put out a sunlight of its own with hundreds and hundreds of blooming goldenrod. Or they'd speak of the crisp white silence of winter when icicles hung like rainbowed glass from all the twigs, and how dear it was to be snuggled away in cozy little homes with a well-stocked pantry.

Sometimes Little Mocker, full of his newfound knowledge of the Keeper and wishing to contribute something enlightening, would ask his visitor if he knew the Keeper. They all did. Some would bow in quiet reverence. Others would nod and let the bright knowledge shine from their eyes unabashedly. Still others said they were glad Little Mocker had become a link in the Keeper's chain.

Over and over Chipmunk, in his tumbling language, would try to tell Little Mocker what life was like "in these hereabouts" as he called it. "You take sundown about time when whipperin' are the poor wills and red is the Deep Forest that comes up over the big wagonwheel moon. Never a time better. Everybody's another good day had and home goes to supper and rest."

Little Mocker would bat his eyes and try to straighten out Chipmunk's talk, but even if he couldn't get all the words in their proper place, he got the idea from Chipmunk's look of peace and contentment that hereabouts was a nice place to live.

While his education and vocabulary grew rapidly by these visits with the talkative ones, Little Mocker also enjoyed and learned from the ones who didn't have much to say. Take Rabbit. Sometimes Rabbit would come and sit in a spot where it was easy for Little Mocker to see him, flick his ears in greeting, and not say a thing out loud. But just the way Rabbit sat, eager and attentive, seemed to say, "I'm here. I'm your friend. Isn't it a good day? Isn't it great to be alive? If ever I can help—" Thus, Little Mocker learned the subtleties of friendship and the comfort of silence.

One day, feeling very good and following Mrs. Raccoon's advice about not being afraid to question, he asked her, "Will you teach me to sing?"

"Singing is not a strong talent of the raccoon," Mrs. Raccoon readily admitted. "This is the best I can do." She hummed a few bars of *Puddin' Doodle*.

Although he didn't say so, Little Mocker had to agree that singing was not a strong point for a raccoon. Squalling maybe, but definitely not singing.

"Maybe you can do it on your own without any lessons," Mrs. Raccoon suggested.

Try as he might, Little Mocker couldn't produce anything that sounded much better than Mrs. Raccoon's squalling. It came out "Che-che-cheep-chee," with no variance in tone, no lilt, no trill, no resonance. Quite depressing. At times he felt the stinging tears brimming his eyes. When this happened, Mrs. Raccoon would take the little tin bucket from the shelf and serve a delightful mixture of meadow seeds. Soon the tears would go away, and Little Mocker would speak freely of his desire to be the best singer in—well, maybe in the whole world. Quite often the way the words came out sounded boastful and as if he thought too much of himself, and he'd apologize for his highfalutin ideas. But Mrs. Raccoon was always hasty to say he was right. "Aim to be the best at everything you do, and you'll be surprised at how close you come."

At last the day came for the removal of the splints. Mr. Raccoon sat by watchfully as Mrs. Raccoon unwound the wool with her deft little fingers. "Now then," she said, "try to flap the wing."

Little Mocker did as told and oh, joy of joys, he could flap it and it didn't hurt a bit. Immediately he backed his stubby tail feathers, which weren't so stubby anymore, against one side of the room and flew to the other side with no effort or pain at all. Of course it was only three wing flaps distance, but at least he didn't go around in circles as he had with only one good wing.

"I guess he is ready to go," Mrs. Raccoon said to her mate.

"I guess so," Mr. Raccoon agreed.

It was almost as if they were bidding good-bye to

one of their own children who was ready to make his way out into the world. But from long experience they both knew that changes had to come. It was as natural as the sun rising in the morning and setting at night.

Little Mocker felt that he must say something, but even with all the things he had learned in recent weeks, he didn't know what to say. A mere "Thank you" didn't seem enough for all the kindness he had been shown. But if he said more, he might be running the risk of chattering like Squirrel. He decided on a jaunty "See you again." Hopping to the doorway, he was about to spread his wings for flight when he noticed the crowd gathered below. Mrs. Raccoon had told some of the neighbours that this might be the day Little Mocker would fly away, and there they all were—frogs and toads, seventy-two meadow mice, Mother 'Possum and babies, Skunky, blue jays, Chuck, Rabbit, Chipmunk. There were even some Little Mocker hadn't met before. Old Beaver had come over from the Shining River, and Terrapin had slow-poked his way from the far end of the Grassy Meadow. They clapped their paws and flapped their wings and said all manner of nice things about his courage and determination.

This was almost more than Little Mocker could bear. For a moment he considered abandoning his leave-taking. Why not just stay here among these jolly good folks? He teetered with indecision, then flew to a nearby branch to have a second thought. There was more applause from below. He looked back at the rounded doorway of the Raccoon home. Mr. and Mrs. Raccoon were looking at him. Was that a tear in Mrs. Raccoon's eye? He fluttered around on his perch as if to fly back, but at that instant he heard the little breezes blowing across the meadow grass again, their tiny musical words whispering just to him, "Come back, Little Mocker. Come back. Out into the sunshine, the fields, the sky. You must learn to sing. That is your gift. Do not neglect it."

"I won't. I won't," Little Mocker whispered. He looked again at his friends gathered below. They were all lined up in neat little rows now, and Head Frog, standing in front, swung a green rhythmic hand as they sang.

> Farewell, Little Mocker, farewell.
> We've loved you while here you did dwell.
> Be ever a link in the Keeper's chain
> And sometime, somewhere, we'll meet again.

Little Mocker swallowed hard, batted his eyes rapidly, said, "See you again," and flew away.

He really had no notion which way to go, but he felt it would be a kindness to those he left behind to make it appear as if he knew exactly where he was going. So he flew in one direction only, until he was out of sight. Then he stopped to make plans how best to get back to his home surroundings.

It was hard to think with this joy of being able to fly again welling up inside of him every few minutes. It started down at his toenails and shivered deliciously right on up through his body. When it reached the topmost feather on his head, it seemed to pull him by some invisible string straight up into the air where he looped and swerved and rolled and spiraled in an ecstasy of freedom. Then he would somersault downward, alight again, straighten his ruffled feathers, and try to think, only to have the same thing happen over again and again and again.

With all these pleasant interruptions, it was getting near sunset before he had formulated a definite travel plan. To go off in any straight direction like a spoke from a wheel hub might get him someplace quick, but it would be a mighty stroke of luck if he

chose the right direction the first, second, or even forti-
eth time. No, he would make circles around the Grassy
Meadow, gently widening them all the time and someday surely he would spy the waterfall or railroad track.
Then he'd have his bearings and could take off in a
straight line.

Satisfied with his plan, he flew to a bush, looked
all around to see that there were no nearby dead trees
that might fall on him in the night, then tucked his
head beneath his wing to sleep. "Thank you, Keeper,"
he murmured into his feathers. Tomorrow he would be
off!

After Little Mocker had gone, Mr. and Mrs. Raccoon descended the trunk of their white oak home to
visit those gathered below.

"You did a fine job of setting that wing, Mrs. Raccoon," Mother 'Possum complimented, setting off a
noisy outburst of congratulations from the others.
Then, as if they could not say enough good things,
they joined hands and danced in a circle around her,
singing an impromptu little ditty that went something
like this:

> Hooray for Mrs. Dr. Raccoon!
> We will sing to her a tune.
> If we have a wound to mend,
> We will have her to attend.

The seventy-two meadow mice couldn't keep up
with the others, so they formed an inner circle of their
own and did a fancy Irish jig, raising such a cloud of
dust it made the frogs sneeze.

Mrs. Raccoon blushed and said she didn't do any
more than anyone else could have done. But she was so
pleased that she climbed back up to her quarters and
brought down all the food she had stored. Others hur-

ried home and brought back what they had. The stump of the old dead hickory was used for a table, and everyone had a merry good time.

"I hope Little Mocker gets to where he's going," said Head Frog after he had wiped his mouth clean of food.

There was a chorus of "So do I's."

"Didn't he wish to stay here with us?" Rabbit asked.

"In a way, I think he did," said Mrs. Raccoon. "But then, more than anything, he wanted to get back to his mother, who was to start his singing lessons."

"Did anyone warn him about the Next County?" Skunky asked.

"Oh yes, we talked of it quite often," Mrs. Raccoon replied. "But then it's so hard to know where the boundaries of the Next County are."

"Yes, it is that," sighed Chuck who had once ended up there by mistake and had never ceased to report the bad conditions that existed. "Did I ever tell you that they throw their rubbish in the rivers and streams?"

"No!" exclaimed the others, properly horrified.

"Yes, they do," said Chuck. "One can't get a good, clean, pure drink of water anywhere, or see the shining pebbles at the bottom of the brooks. You know where our Rustling Brook flows over the rocks and makes the water fly up like white lace?" Everyone nodded in recognition, for it was a restful place to go and sit and listen to the water music. "Well, you don't see anything like that over there. Just brown water, muddy brown water, with all manner of rubbish floating on top."

Head Frog jumped up with indignation. "No one had better try anything like that with Rustling Brook," he said, batting his bulging eyes threateningly.

"And chewing gum foil and sweet wrappers and paper cups and napkins," Chuck continued. "They just throw them down wherever they happen to be when they are through with them."

There was much clucking of tongues and sad shaking of heads.

Skunky felt that it was too gloomy a way to start a new day. He jumped up on the dead hickory stump, his arm resting at a peculiar angle against his side, and began again to tell how the tree fell. "Here she was, folks, tall and barkless and full of woodpecker homes. Just standing here in the moonlight. Then all at once, Crack-Splat-Slam-Whomp! over she went." He fell very slowly, having practiced this trick for several days. There was such a snapping crushing noise accompanying the fall that the others were truly alarmed. Skunky quivered once or twice, batted his eyes, and slowly closed them.

"Oh, Skunky," breathed Rabbit sadly.

"He's broken a bunch of bones this time," Squirrel announced. "Did you hear them crack?"

"Yes, yes, we heard it quite distinctly," said all the

little meadow mice, who were even farther away from the scene than all the others.

Mrs. Raccoon lifted one of Skunky's eyelids and was surprised at how bright and devilish the eye looked. "Skunky, are you hurt? Skunky?" She tweaked his ear.

At this Skunky got up, laughing, quite alert, and certainly all together.

"How did you make all that noise, Skunky?" asked the frogs, clapping their hands delightedly and thinking it a good joke they might try themselves sometime.

"Oak puff ball," Skunky explained expansively, pulling the remains of a crushed ball from beneath his arm.

"Skunky," warned Mother 'Possum, "you're going to have to have Mrs. Raccoon set a bone for you one of these days if you're not careful."

But Skunky only laughed, thanked Mrs. Raccoon and the others for the party, and went away toward the Deep Forest, already planning how he'd do his act the next time.

7

Mrs. Raccoon Hunts for the Brass Trimmed Box

When the others had gone to be about their day's business, Mr. and Mrs. Raccoon climbed back to their home. There was a feather on the floor they hadn't noticed before.

"Little Mocker's," said Mr. Raccoon, a twinge of sadness in his voice.

Mrs. Raccoon picked it up tenderly and put it on the treasure shelf, placing the edge of the blue Vicks Vapo-rub jar on a tiny portion of it so that it could not blow away. She rearranged the shiny foil balls, dusted

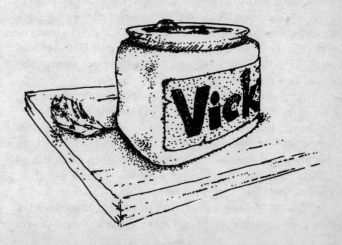

the tab can openers, and for the first time since her hazardous trip to the dump pile remembered the gaily painted box with the brass corners and blinking lights. She started to tell Mr. Raccoon about it, but Mr. Raccoon was already curled up in the bed, half asleep, for raccoons do love a daytime nap.

Perhaps she should take one, too. It had been an eventful morning with Little Mocker's departure and then the picnic party. She lay down, yawned, closed her eyes, but sleep would not come. The vision of the colourful box kept dancing before her eyes. It would be too big to get up to their quarters, but it could be placed in a sheltered place in the hedgerow where she could see it and the others could enjoy it too. That is, if it were still there at the dump pile. Lots of things disappeared from dump piles. The thought propelled her to her feet almost as abruptly as the fall of the big hickory many weeks ago.

Quickly she was out the doorway, down the tree trunk, and on her way to the dump pile, full of excitement, yet fussing at herself for being so foolhardy as to make such an unnecessary daring daytime appearance. At times she even stopped and considered turning back to await darkness, but then the remembered gleam of those shiny brass ornaments would tug at her feet and pull them forward as if attached to puppet strings she could not control.

At the edge of the woods surrounding the dump pile, Mrs. Raccoon paused a long while to study the situation. There was no truck or Man in sight, not even the sounds of a distant motor. Once a small motion at the base of the enormous pile of discarded things caught her attention, but it was only Dump Pile Rat, who called this place his home.

She made her way across the open space and began pawing aside furnace filters, bicycle tyres, petrol

cans, bottles, bashed bags, and battered bushel baskets.
Two hours later, when she was quite deep within the
dump, with all sense of direction gone, she began to
realize what an enormous project she had undertaken.
In the intervening weeks since she had been there,
more and more things had been dumped. For all she
knew, the desired object might be hundreds of feet
below the level where she was searching.

Just as she was about ready to give up for the day
and try to find her way back out, she saw what appeared to be blinking lights and started toward them in
a hurry, only to discover they were the eyes of Dump
Pile Rat. "Oh, it's you, D.P.," Mrs. Raccoon said.

"How do you do? Welcome to my castle," said D.P.
very graciously.

"D.P., I'm looking for something," explained Mrs.
Raccoon, and told him all about the bright box with
lights and brass trimmings. "Have you seen such a
thing?"

D.P. scratched his head. His brow furrowed with the
effort of thinking. "There is so much, you know. It really
taxes me to keep an up-to-date inventory. Right now, such
an object does not come readily to my mind. But I can
give you a guided tour. Perhaps you have not seen the
brass bedstead that came in recently, or the three by six
flowered linoleum, the blue granite coffeepot, the newest
orange crate, the unbroken blue Mason jar.

"Oh, D.P., let's get started," Mrs. Raccoon interrupted, knowing the list could go on and on for days
and days.

"Well, let's see," mused D.P. "The east wing is not
open now, due to a smouldering fire, so we had better
start this way." He disappeared into a nearby tunnel
between a Hi-C grape juice can and a rusty alarm
clock.

Mrs. Raccoon attempted to follow, but the hallway

was much too small for her. The Hi-C can became dislodged, which in turn turned over the alarm clock, which let loose a one-runnered sled that was anchoring a split-open featherbed. "Oh my, oh my," she wailed in dismay. "What have I done? D.P.!" she called out. But her voice was lost in the rattle, clang, thud, squooge, squinch, and squonk that followed.

When all had fallen that was going to fall, which took a good five minutes, Mrs. Raccoon found herself sitting on a xylophone on the surface of the dump pile in the late afternoon sunshine. There were feathers in her mouth, ears, eyes, sticking to her nose, and embedded in her fur all the way to the tip of her seven-ringed tail.

While she was still spitting feathers, D.P. thrust his head through the rearranged outer surface nearby. Feathers adorned his whiskers on each side of his mouth, and one stood straight up atop each ear, giving him such a comical appearance Mrs. Raccoon stopped her own de-feathering, helpless with uncontrollable laughter.

D.P. was so seldom the cause of gaiety that he enjoyed this immensely and struck several poses as if he were being photographed for a high-fashion magazine cover.

When she could talk again, Mrs. Raccoon began to apologize. "D.P., I'm afraid I have destroyed some of your hallways. I am sorry."

"Oh, think nothing of it," D.P. replied. "'Tis spring and if there is anything I like, it's a little bit of redecoration in spring. That particular tunnel has been in existence since last October. Time for re-routing."

By sundown they had divested themselves of all feathers and sleeked their fur.

"D.P., it is apparent that my size does not accommodate itself to your tunnels," Mrs. Raccoon said.

D.P. pulled at his whiskers in a most solemn manner and agreed that that did seem to be perfectly clear.

"So, it will be a great favour for me, if in your rambles through your, uh, castle, you will be on the lookout for this box."

"Certainly, certainly," D.P. said. "But it would be of help if you could give me some general clue as to its location. About where were you before when you first found it?"

Mrs. Raccoon looked around for landmarks. "I was so scared, D.P., that all I could think of was getting back home without losing my tail. Chuck was with me, and he came out first. Let's see. Yes, I believe it was about over there where that old stove is now. Yes, it was about there, for I remember making a hasty run toward that patch of sassafras brush."

"Then I shall begin this very night to explore," promised D.P.

8
Little Mocker Lands in the Next County

At the end of the first week after Little Mocker's departure from the Grassy Meadow, he was only about ten miles away, although he had covered considerable territory. As planned, he had flown in ever widening circles around the Grassy Meadow, but nowhere had he caught a glimpse of a railroad track or a waterfall.

Now it was another bright dazzling morning, and he was eager to be off. The sun was making miniature rainbows in the dewdrops hanging from every blade of grass. The little breezes whispered, "Wonderful day. Wonderful day," in their most musical voices. The air was spicy with mingled scents. Little Mocker flitted around on his perch, getting a good look at the world from all directions. There was such a terrible excitement in his breast as he thought of what the new day might hold. There would be new vistas, possibly new acquaintances, and maybe a reunion with his family in time to learn a few notes of the mockingbird scale.

By midmorning he had crossed a large field where a Man was ploughing, a wide pasture dotted with black and white cows, a patch of pines, and a thickly wooded hill. At the foot of the far side of the hill he spied a stream of water and, being thirsty, stopped for a drink. The bank was muddy and littered with rusty cans and broken bottles. He picked his way carefully through the rubbish so as not to injure a toe. He had to wait a while for a plastic bleach bottle to float past before he could dip his beak into the water. When it was gone, there came an oil can, followed by six beer cans, a one-eyed doll, a piece of driftwood, a fishing cork, three paper cups, and a dead fish. In fact, Little Mocker soon learned that if he were to get a drink at all, he'd just have to be quick about it, dipping his beak in between floating objects.

The water didn't taste good. Furthermore, it smelled bad. He hopped back up the bank and flew to a scraggly looking bush, an uneasiness that he did not understand beginning to stir somewhere down deep inside. While he was perching there trying to account for his sudden low feeling, a movement in a nearby bush caught his eyes. Cocking his head first one way, then the other, he soon saw that it was another bird. Quickly he flew to the same bush and said in a most polite way, "Good-day."

"What's good about it?" came back a grouchy answer.

Little Mocker began to relate all the good things that he had seen and felt.

"Oh, bosh!" interrupted the stranger.

Little Mocker didn't know exactly what this meant, but he felt that it wasn't friendly. After a while he said, "My name is Little Mocker," and waited for the other bird to state his name. When he didn't, Little Mocker continued, "I'm trying to find my mother so as to start my singing lessons."

There was a short silence broken at length by a burst of derisive laughter. "Singing lessons?" said the stranger. He eyed Little Mocker with disbelief. "Singing lessons?" he repeated, and went off into another gale of contemptuous laughter.

This was the first time Little Mocker had ever felt

the sting of ridicule. It gave him a crawly feeling at the base of his neck. The water he had just drunk was beginning to make him sick too. "Well, how else could I learn to sing?" he asked, a little more saucy than he felt was good manners.

"Steal your notes. Rip 'em right out of the air!"

"Steal? Rip?" Little Mocker said. "I don't think I understand."

But the stranger, having seen a morsel of food floating by on the crowded waters, dived swiftly toward it, only to collide with another bird who had seen the morsel too. There followed a fight such as Little Mocker had never before witnessed. For a moment or two, there was nothing but a blur of feathers, a tangle of beaks and claws, twirling, whirling, and screeching. Suddenly the two birds took off downstream, evidently in search of the food that had floated on by. In a little while Little Mocker heard the angry cries again and supposed they had rediscovered the bit of food.

He flew across the bad smelling stream and landed in another bush. The sick feeling in the pit of his stomach intensified. Perhaps, he thought, if I had something to eat, I'd feel better. He looked around, then flew down to walk alongside the stream for a while, hoping another morsel of food might come drifting by. All he saw was another dead fish. Quickly he lifted his wings and flew away, preferring to go hungry rather than eat a dead fish.

A little way beyond the stream he came to a hedgerow where he found a few shriveled rosehips. He ate them and felt a little better. High overhead he noticed a hawk soaring in big lazy circles. How effortlessly he seemed to move. If I were only up there, I could see more, find my way better, thought Little Mocker, and marveled that he had not thought of this before. He set his wings and began an upward climb, but by the time he was treetop high his body began to dip forward and he had to flap his wings very fast to keep from taking a nosedive into the ground. Time after time he tried it, and the same thing happened. On his last trial he straightened out just in time to avoid hitting the ground, or rather a moving object on the ground. When his head had cleared and he could focus on the moving object, Little Mocker's heart gave a great leap of joy. "Mrs. Raccoon," he shouted.

"Buzz off, Boob," replied the raccoon, giving Little Mocker such a strong cuff to the face it sent him reeling backwards.

When he righted himself, he looked at the departing raccoon and saw that he had made a mistake. There were only five rings in its tail, and the rest of its fur didn't look as though it had been groomed in the last ten years.

Little Mocker spent the next half hour wearily flitting about in the hedgerow, accomplishing nothing. Two meadow mice went strolling by, and didn't so much as look in his direction although he spoke to them and wished them a good day. Off in the distance he heard a woodpecker. The rappings sounded harsh and hurt his head, which was beginning to ache fiercely. A strange darkness seemed to be spreading over the land. He looked at the sun and saw that it was only midafternoon. But everything seemed to be getting smaller and smaller, receding into little pinpoints of light and finally total darkness.

My eyes!" Little Mocker cried aloud. "Something is wrong with my eyes!" He heard a noise nearby and called out again that something was wrong with his eyes, hoping whoever made the noise would come to his aid. No one did, even though he heard footsteps and a swish of wings several times.

Since the blow that the strange raccoon had given

him was the first cuff Little Mocker had ever had about the head, he had no way of knowing that this was a temporary blindness caused by his eyes swelling shut. He thought that he had had his last look at the beautiful world. No more dew rainbows in the grass. No more windflowers nodding in the breeze. No more fleecy white clouds in a blue sky. He slid down, down into a black pit of despair, wishing that the earth would soak him in like so many raindrops.

As he was lying there utterly dejected, he failed to hear the softly approaching footsteps, the low guttural growl, the spitting and hissing of some hungry creature. But he did feel the grip of teeth about his neck. At first he did not protest, hoping that another kindly creature like Mrs. Raccoon had come to carry him away to safety.

When the teeth sank so far as to bring a stab of pain, Little Mocker protested loudly, flapped his wings, and managed to get away. But only for a short while, for in his blindness he flew into a tree trunk, stunned himself, and fell to the ground. Quickly the unknown, unseen creature was upon him. This time it had him by a wing and was twirling him about wildly. Luckily a few feathers broke, and Little Mocker managed to escape again. He rose into the air and began to fly willy-nilly, for some important wing feathers had been broken and he felt, for he could not actually see, that he was going in a circle again, as he had back in Mrs. Raccoon's home with the broken wing, and sliding sideways. The puncture in his neck was hurting very badly. Sometimes his wingtips brushed against tree branches or tall weeds or grass, he couldn't really tell what. When he felt he was no longer able to keep altitude, he set his wings and went for a landing—where he did not know.

It was fortunate that he landed in the middle of the muddy stream, for he was moving with much more speed than he would have had he been able to see. A ground landing at such speed would have been the end of Little Mocker. As it was, there was only a loud splash and a change of course for a massed collection of floating beer cans.

He came up spluttering, a wet mass of feathers, slimy weeds draped around his neck and green bubbly algae decorating each wing tip. Carefully he crawled to the top of a can, only to have it roll and sink, and him with it. This happened time after time, for Little Mocker could not see what he was doing. Finally, through what he later felt in his heart to be an intervention by the great Keeper of All Creatures, he came up out of the water and climbed on something which, although he couldn't tell at the time, proved to be a floating plank, wide and stable enough for him to maintain balance. He lay sprawled, wings outstretched, toenails curled under, blind. He alternately gasped and choked and coughed and croaked until the water was out of his lungs and he was breathing easy again.

How long he lay there, weak and helpless, floating downstream, Little Mocker did not know. Visions of the soft dry comfort of Mrs. Raccoon's Flower Garden quilt, her little bucket of meadow seed, Skunky telling about the fall of the hickory, Rabbit sitting nearby with his wise eyes and expressive ears, passed through his mind. Why, oh why, had he ever left such a wonderful place? Where, oh where was he now?

Then, with the particular clarity that sometimes comes when darkness is all about and one has plumbed the depths of despair, he knew at once, with great certainty, and said out loud, "I am in the Next County." A shiver of some unnamed fear passed over his body. "Oh, Keeper," he whimpered.

9
Little Mocker Sings

Little Mocker flopped himself about on the board until he found its edge. Tentatively he let one foot fall over and touch the water. How easy it would be to just roll over and let himself sink to the bottom. Not only easy, but desirable. Never again to see, never to sing, and in the dreaded Next County without wing power to fly out! He edged closer and closer, finding a certain peace in the idea of ending all his misery and failure.

Vaguely and seemingly from somewhere far away, he heard the voice of an owl, "Who, who? To who?"

"Oh, who, who, to who yourself," answered Little Mocker with a bravado that sometimes identifies those who have come to the limit of their fear and despair.

And then a wonderful thing happened. Down through the misery of his fear, the jagged points of pain in his sore neck and tired wings, Little Mocker realized he had sounded just like the owl.

With lightning speed he withdrew his foot from the water and rolled back a few inches from the perilous edge, all his hopelessness of the moment before swept away as by some swift wind. He lay trembling all over, but this time it was with delight. He had struck a true note in the musical scale. Very low, to be sure, but true and soft and velvety. He had—why, he had literally *stolen* the notes of the owl. He felt giddy with power. He had ripped 'em right out of the air where the owl had put them. And if he could do this with the notes of one bird, why not many? Why not all?

In spite of his wetness, Little Mocker felt light and beautiful and spent the next few hours reveling in his old dream of being able to fly through the air, making fancy loops and circles, climbs and dives, leaving a golden chain of rich melody floating in his wake. He no longer felt the pain in his neck, the tiredness of his body. He forgot that he could not see.

In a predawn hour he heard some clear whistled phrases of two or three notes, rich and happy as if whoever were making them thought that the prospect of a new day coming was the richest gift one could possess. After he had listened to the phrases a time or two, Little Mocker opened his mouth and out they came, "Teea lo lolay, tolay, toly, teealo." A perfect copy. Then he opened his eyes, and he could see. Dirty and polluted as the water was, his dip into its coolness had caused the swelling to go away. He repeated the song over and over as his own paean of praise for all his blessings. He could see! He could sing! There was the world before him. Not the beautiful Grassy Meadow, the clear Rustling Brook, the fragrant hedgerow, but the world. He saw that he was still on his plank raft, but

72

no longer moving. It had lodged against the bank in a conglomeration of other miscellaneous debris. He remembered his experience in the night and quickly tried out his other song, "Who, who, to-who?" It came out with perfect pitch and resonance. He put the two songs together, first one way, then another.

A dead fish went floating close by, and this time Little Mocker reached out and caught it in his beak. Distasteful as it might be, he knew he had to eat something to put strength back into his body. When he had eaten and rested again, he went about cleaning his body. Then he squatted down and spread his wings out wide so the warmth of the climbing sun would hasten the drying. He saw that one wing did not look right. Three of his main flight feathers did not spread in place. He raised the wing. The same feathers hung down frazzled and defeated. He tried to flip them back in place, but they would not go. He craned his neck closer and saw that the feathers were broken about halfway down the center shaft.

Had he not been so happy over the fact that he could see again and also sing, Little Mocker probably would have sunk into another morass of despair. As it was, he quickly mounted into the air to test his flight. He did not get very far, for the injured wing could not balance the power of the other wing, and he soon found himself in the slimy stream again. Scrabbling to the plank, he fluttered and preened and after a while tried again to fly. But it was into the river and out again.

"Now what I will have to do," he said to himself, in the same organizational voice he'd heard Mr. Raccoon use so much, "is to get off this plank, climb onto the bank, get to a branch somewhere, and dry out."

It took him most of the morning to accomplish this. While still on the bank, the same scruffy raccoon he had encountered the previous day came by. Little Mocker crouched low in the riverbank weeds lest he be seen, thinking what a terrible thing it was to have to hide from someone.

When he felt it was safe, he scooted along the ground as fast as he could. The dangling feathers caught on things and jerked him sideways. He tried mounting into the air again and found that even if he couldn't get very high and could only go a few feet at a time before having to make a most awkward landing, he did make faster progress.

Seeing a sapling with low growing branches, Little Mocker aimed for it. Such crippled flying was tiring, and by the time he reached a branch where the sun might shine on him again, he was gasping for breath. But it didn't matter, not one bit, for somewhere nearby another song was being poured into the air.

It was the most beautiful thing Little Mocker had ever heard. There was a flutelike opening, long, low, and silvery. Then a trill of a dozen or more notes, light as milkweed floss, airy, bell-like, all run together in a tremolo of exaltation, now near, now fading away as if the notes were being carried away by ethereal bodies above the treetops, above the clouds, into the very heavens for an offering of sweet incense to the Keeper of All Creatures.

Just as the last notes faded away, the whole thing was repeated. Little Mocker closed his eyes and shivered as the pure liquid gold of the notes was so freely, so generously emptied into the air. He wished to repeat them immediately to see if he could, but wondered if he should. This bird of the beautiful song might be angry, might not sing in his presence again.

He kept his eyes on the bush from which the song was coming. Soon there was a little flurry of motion, and a bird flew out and away.

"Come back," Little Mocker called. "Come back. Please do come back."

But the bird of the beautiful song evidently did not hear, for it never so much as dipped a wing in his direction. Little Mocker watched until it became a mere speck in the sky and then disappeared entirely.

He tried the first flutelike notes, raised them higher, too high, lowered them again until they came out just as he had heard them. Then he did the trill, and the tremolo. In no time at all he had it in all its perfect glory. Over and over he sang, making the area around him ring with gladness. He put it together with the other songs and calls he had learned, rearranged them, putting a "Who, who, to-who," right in the middle of a "teea lo lolay, tolay."

When he paused to get his breath for another outburst, he heard someone shout in a raucous voice, "Hey, Scraggly, knock it off. I gotta get some sleep."

Little Mocker looked down and saw a muddy-haired fox lolling lazily on the ground. "I'm sorry," he said respectfully, although smarting from the name he had been called. He looked at his drooping wing feathers, tried to pull them back in place, but could not move them an inch.

"Do you live right here?" Little Mocker asked, looking around for a den or log or stump that must serve as the fox's home.

"I live anywhere I please," came the snappy reply.

Little Mocker did not try to make any further conversation. When he thought the fox was asleep, he hopped to a higher branch, and then to one a little higher until he came to the topmost branch of the sapling. From there, with much effort of hopping and fluttery flying, he transferred to the branch of a dog-wood tree, and from there, branch by branch, to the top of a tall elm. He wanted to get as high as he could so he might have a better look at his surroundings and make some plans for his immediate future.

From the top of the elm he got a good look at the countryside. It was a sorry-looking sight. There was the muddy, winding river full of floating rubble, the stinking odour of which assailed his nostrils even at this height. The floor of the woods was not much cleaner. To his right two creatures were engaged in a terrible, ripping, slashing fight. There was such a blur of movement and flying of fur he could not tell what they were. To his left, some crows were eating from a shattered rabbit carcass. Along the riverbank, he saw the raccoon with the five-ringed tail making his way, cuffing rabbits, rats, and other raccoons out of his way. It was all most depressing.

He was going to have to be wary and wily to survive in this horrible place where kindness and decency and order seemed unknown.

About a hundred feet away he saw what must at one time have been a fence. Here and there was some sagging, rusting wire and a rotten fencepost or two; but long ago briars, thistles, and vines had taken over, and the whole thing was the wildest of thickets. Little Mocker thought it might provide shelter and food. Carefully he descended and slowly made his way there.

It was afternoon when he arrived. He hopped and fluttered up to a place that was densely screened and leaned wearily against an interlacing of vines. This could be home for a while, he thought. It was not a happy thought. Even though he had discovered that he could sing without benefit of lessons, if no one wanted to hear him, what good would it do?

10
D.P. Rat Finds the Brass Trimmed Box

It was about two months after Dump Pile Rat had begun his search for the brightly painted, brass cornered box with flashing lights before he found it. He had been most diligent and systematic, mentally dividing the dump into sections and storeys. But with all the new rubbish coming in almost every day, rearranging his alleys, tunnels, and division markers, it was hard to keep from repeating or maybe even skipping some places.

One day after a particularly big load had been dumped and long after things should have settled down and stopped squeaking and squawking, something continued to make a noise, a sort of "lo-lo-lo-lo" sound. At first D.P. thought that one of his friends had been caught in a crunch. Quickly he made his way around old table legs, catalogues, horse collars, telephone books, and such in the direction of the noise. He had to stop often and redirect himself, for the echoes within his mighty castle were very misleading. Once he came upon a room he had long forgotten and wished he could have lingered. It was a cozy little room inside a large wooden box which he had floored with a piece of shag rug. There was a neat little bed and a cupboard for cheese. But he felt he had to hurry on in the direction of the noise, which now seemed more like a rhythmic heartbeat somewhere deep in the dump rather than a cry of pain or panic.

Somehow, and certainly without meaning to, he got into some coily bedsprings and spent a good part of an hour getting out. Round and round he went, over and over the same old trail. It was most aggravating until finally it occurred to him that if he went in one straight direction between the coils he'd have to come to the edge. Bedsprings didn't cover the whole world. Once out, he rounded a rusty country-style mailbox, climbed over a half-used ball of binder twine, and came upon the thing that was making the noise. It was Mrs. Raccoon's box.

There were no flashing lights, but he recognized it from the ornamental brass corners Mrs. Raccoon had described and the bright colors. There were lots of little knobs, buttons, and slots. Painted pictures of butterflies, owls, kittens, kites, and kangaroos decorated the sides. He pushed one of the buttons, and immediately blue lights began to flash through the owl eyes. It startled him so, he fell back into a rusty flour sieve and had a terrible time extricating himself. When he did, he pushed the button again and the lights went out. He pushed another button and the "lo-lo-lo-lo" stopped. He pushed it again and the sound came back. "I say, now. This is a jolly contraption," he exclaimed. He pushed other buttons, pulled levers, turned cranks; but all he could get was the blue lights and the "lo-lo-lo-lo."

On one side there seemed to be some printing, but D.P. couldn't read.

He pushed at the box with both front paws, testing its weight, and was surprised that he couldn't move it an inch. He leaped at it with all four paws with no better results. Then he tried to lift a corner of it, and all he did was break one of his toenails.

"By Jiminy, this might be more of a problem than

I thought." He tweaked his whiskers, scratched his head, and settled back, hands behind head, to study the matter.

Certainly he'd need help to move the thing. How much, he didn't know. It might take both Mr. and Mrs. Raccoon and Mother 'Possum and Skunky and Rabbit and Squirrel and Chuck. "Whoa!" he said, stopping his own plans. Rabbit and Squirrel and Skunky didn't like coming into the internal parts of the dump. Mother 'Possum would have to get baby-sitters. Mr. and Mrs. Raccoon might be willing since she seemed so desirous of the thing, but, remembering the great avalanche Mrs. Raccoon had caused the last time she tried to fit herself into his tunnels, D.P. thought it unwise to try that again. In fact, he supposed no tunnel would work, however carefully constructed and braced, for with the moving of the box there would be so much disturbing of delicately balanced things, avalanche after avalanche would occur.

After much thought, D.P. felt that the only safe way to get the box out would be to tie a rope around it, thread the rope through a tunnel to the outside, and get all his friends to pull from the outside. It would take tremendous pull power, for no doubt the box would get lodged and tangled and maybe, for all he knew, had a mind of its own that would be obstinate.

In addition to Mr. and Mrs. Raccoon, Squirrel, Skunky, Chuck, and Rabbit, it might take all the frogs and meadow mice. "Hmmm" he thought, "I wonder how much mouse power we have now."

D.P. didn't mean to take a nap, but counting the meadow mice was most conducive to sleep. He began with the boys. "Raymond, Fred, Robert, Jonathan, Carswell, Gary, Jack, Scott, Joe, Edward, Med, Ned, Stephen, Earl, Curtis, Wilson." Then he switched to the girls. "Bess, Ruthie, Dorothy, Lillian, Pearl, Lou,

Margaret, Pat, Thomza, Peggy, Rebecca, Gladys." Tiring of that he alternated the boys and girls. "David, Alice, Calvin, Nellie, Charles, Kathleen, Todd, Camilla, Moses, Gerry—"

D.P. was on fifty when he drifted off to sleep. When he awoke an hour later, he resumed his counting until he reached one hundred and fifteen. He could not think of another single one, although he hadn't been up to the Grassy Meadow lately. One hundred and fifteen mousepower plus all the others. That ought to do it.

He started his exit by the way he had come, but remembering the perplexity of the bedsprings decided on another route. He was well past a furnace filter, a beaten-up briefcase, and a cracked crock when the thought struck him that with all the shifting and changing that occurred in the dump, he might not be able to find his way back. He needed definite, well-defined landmarks. One cracked crock looked just like another cracked crock, and coffee cans were alike as peas in a pod.

"What I need is a long string to mark my trail." He poked around at the nearby accumulation, then suddenly remembered the binder twine. Hurriedly he found it, tied the loose end to the brass cornered box, and began winding his way out of the dump, pulling the twine along gently behind him so as not to break the trail.

It took him ten minutes before he emerged into bright daylight. About fifty feet from the dump he scratched a hole, buried the remainder of the twine, and placed a pile of rocks on top for a marker. Then he started at a rapid pace to tell Mrs. Raccoon.

11
Skunky Gets Caught in a Trap

D.P. had not gone far before he noticed an omi-silence. At this season of the year there was usually plenty of sound in both woods and clearings. He stopped to listen intently. No bird sang. No cricket chirruped. No squirrel chattered. It gave him a strange feeling, as if he had suddenly been transported to another world. Or maybe gone deaf! He scratched at a log for a quick test and was relieved that he could hear the noise he made.

When he passed Chuck's house he darted inside, but Chuck was not at home. From the looks of the place he had left in a hurry, leaving his bed unmade and some crumbs on the floor.

A little farther along, D.P.'s eyes became adjusted to distances, and he noticed slight movements here and there—the bending of some grass, a flutter of leaves. Soon he was able to detect silent forms stealthily moving along, all in one direction, toward the Grassy Meadow. He hurried to catch up with Chipmunk, who was half walking, half running, but very carefully, so as not to snap a twig or crackle a dry leaf.

"What's up, Chip?" he asked.

"Shh!" whispered Chip, clamping a hand over his mouth to indicate silence was now necessary.

"What's up, Chip?" D.P. asked again, in a hoarse whisper.

"Skunky. He's in a trap been caught!"

"Skunky? In whose trap? Where? Is he hurt?"

"Over by the cornfield, third fencepost north from the big cottonwood," Chipmunk answered. "We've got quiet to be so as Dog not to arouse."

"Can we get him out?" D.P. asked softly. This business of traps was grave.

"Word's been spread, and everybody's going to see what can be done," Chipmunk replied, beginning to calm a little.

The two friends crept along as silently as they could. Soon they were joined by Chuck and Rabbit and a dozen or so meadow mice, all very sober and downcast.

"Oh my," said Rabbit, being the first to get a whiff of Skunky's protective perfume.

"Gellikee whiskers," moaned Chuck when the scent reached his nose.

The meadow mice, marching single-file, fell back like a row of toppled dominoes.

"We've just got to go on," whispered Rabbit. "No matter how strong this becomes."

D.P. and Chuck nodded in agreement, and the meadow mice said, quite faintly, "We's all will come soon as we can." A few of them wobbled to their feet, but fell back again upon taking a deep breath.

The scent got stronger and stronger as they hurried along, which was a good way of knowing they were going in the right direction. When they arrived at the third fencepost north of the cottonwood, there was a frantic but silent commotion going on. Everyone who was already there was pulling and tugging at various parts of the boxlike trap, hoping to find some weak spot so as to make an opening for Skunky to escape.

Mr. Raccoon pulled at one side, which was made of chicken wire. Mrs. Raccoon pulled at the opposite side. Mother 'Possum prised helplessly at a nail in the wooden end.

Chipmunk, when he arrived, picked up a stout stick and tried to turn the whole thing over to see if there might be a door in the floor.

D.P., having had such a recent experience with levers and knobs, began to poke at knots in the wood and to pull at splinters.

Skunky, shivering and quivering, looked all folded up, for the trap was very tight quarters for him. His tail was pushed down flat over his back, and his front feet and back feet seemed to be growing out of the same ankles.

"Skunky," whispered Mrs. Raccoon, "is there anything in there to push or pull?"

"I don't know," said Skunky in a very shaky voice, although he was trying his very best to be brave. "I just walked in here and 'Slam!' that end fell down and it scared me, and so I—well, when I'm scared, I—"

"We know, Skunky, we know," said Mrs. Raccoon kindly. "Never mind that. Just look around and see if there is anything to move."

At this point, Chipmunk was successful in turning the trap over and everyone went sprawling. Now Skunky was upside down and somehow or other two meadow mice who had bravely made their way to the scene had become squeezed in the trap with him, one with a grazed nose.

"Oh, my! I never in all my life meant for this to happen," exclaimed Chipmunk. "I only wanted there might be door to see the bottom to get out of, but some way I'll turn it over back." He picked up his stout stick and began to right the trap.

It was no trouble for the meadow mice to crawl out through the wire, but they were so upset by the sudden displacement, they ran around in circles making little squeaky sounds.

Finally Mr. Raccoon said in a hushed but still authorative voice, "Now what we must do is calm down and go at this in an organized manner. Squirrel, you go up that tree and keep a lookout. Someone go get Beaver. Maybe he can chew a hole somewhere. You meadow mice," for they had all arrived by this time, "line up over there out of the way for a while."

By this time Skunky had managed to twist and turn himself over until he was right side up in the upside down cage.

"It's all my fault," wailed Rabbit. "That trap was meant for me."

"That doesn't make it your fault," Mrs. Raccoon protested. She gave a mighty pull at the chicken wire, which only made the holes stretch into narrow horizontal slits.

"But if it wasn't for me and members of my family, that trap wouldn't be there." Rabbit continued hopping around in a most frustrated manner.

"Skunky, how come you wandered into a rabbit

trap, anyway?" asked Chuck, who had just discovered a chain leading away from the trap.

Skunky mumbled something which no one heard nor asked him to repeat. He was in there and that was that. What was more, as Chuck was just discovering, the chain was fastened to a post hammered into the ground.

"D.P., you got any wire cutters or crowbars at the dump?" asked Mr. Raccoon.

No one heard D.P.'s answer, for at that moment Squirrel shouted from his treetop perch, "Dog's coming!"

A paralyzing fear clamped down on the crowd. The frogs turned a shade greener. The meadow mice trembled. Rabbit flattened out on the ground. Mother 'Possum curled up in a ball and tried to look as if she wasn't there. Mrs. Raccoon very disconnectedly said, "Oh, Keeper—now—strength—Skunky—trap—help—protect—thank you." All the while, the distant barking of Dog got nearer and nearer.

Mr. Raccoon was the first to recover. "We've got to pull together and take the whole trap!" he shouted, throwing silence to the wind. "Take hold, everyone, and heave ho!" He grasped the chain firmly in his hands while all the rest lined up and pulled on the link in front of him as for a tug of war.

"Pull!" he called again. The post moved a little more.

"Pull!" he called again.

Soon everyone was calling, "Pull! Pull! Pull!" in a rhythm and resoluteness that left no room for defeat.

In between "Pulls!" Squirrel was tracing aloud the approach of Dog. "He's by the wheat field. He's by the rail fence. Now he's passed the sugar grove. He's coming alongside this field!"

At this point in Squirrel's account, Rabbit, with a look of grim determination, slipped out of place and made for the edge of the field where Dog was coming.

On about the twenty-third concerted pull, the post came flying out of the ground. On lesser occasion there would have been much laughter at the fabulous falls and flying sprawls caused by the sudden release of the post. But now everyone righted himself quickly and began to get away from that place.

Mr. and Mrs. Raccoon and Chuck, holding the chain with the trapped Skunky dragging behind, began running as fast as they could. The others ran alongside, shouting encouragement and lending a hand when the trap got hung on a bush or between rocks.

Bumpety-bump, clink, clank, clunk! Never had Skunky had such a rough ride. The trap slammed up against a boulder, jarring his teeth. A sharp pointed stick came through the wire and stabbed him in the chest. Now on his side, now on his back, tail up, tail down, nose slammed against the trap end, legs tangled, head bumped, soon he was so dizzy the whole forest seemed to be spinning around him. Through a cottony fog of giddiness and pain he heard someone say, "Where you taking him?" And someone answered, "To the dump. We'll hide him in the trash until we can figure out something."

Skunky was glad they had not abandoned him to Dog, but—"Ouch, oooh!"—a thorn ripped his fur on his right side, a briar raked his left. Then, "Blunk!" there was an abrupt stop. The trap hit a log, and a link of the chain anchored on a knot.

"Pull, pull, pull," came frantic orders from the other side of the log, and all the friends ran up front to pull.

Soon the trap was over the log, and the chain loosed. A cheer went up, and the race continued.

But something else had happened. The wooden end of the trap, having been battered and bumped, nicked and knocked, scraped and scratched, suddenly, with the one mighty pull, gave way. Skunky was unceremoniously dumped on the ground almost underneath the log. He was quite weak and breathless and half-covered with old leaves and torn-up moss.

Since all his friends were over the log, out of sight, they did not notice what had happened.

"Not much farther," said D.P. who was guiding the entourage by the shortest shortcut he knew.

Rounding a clump of hazelnut bushes, Mr. and Mrs. Raccoon and all the others leading the rescue tumbled over Beaver, who was late to receive the word and was just now on his way to the big cottonwood.

"Could you inform me of what is going on?" Beaver asked after everyone had righted himself.

"No time to tell, Beav. Just grab hold and help us get Skunky to the dump," said Mr. Raccoon.

Beaver grabbed hold, but inquired of Chuck, "Where is Skunky?"

"In the trap. And Dog was coming too quick, and after dogs come sticks that bark fire," replied Chuck.

"I see," said Beaver. But he really didn't see, for he had taken a good look at the trap and couldn't see Skunky anywhere. After a while, when they were within sight of the dump, he ventured to say, "Does the trap have a secret compartment?"

"No, of course not," said Chuck, out of breath. "J-j-just an old homemade rab-b-b-bit trap. But we couldn't get it opened, so had to bring Skunky along inside."

Beaver's brow wrinkled. He looked back again at the trap, which was now quite twisted and splintered. "I beg your pardon, Chuck. But it does appear to me that Skunky is no longer in the trap."

Chuck looked back, and to his amazement Beaver was right. Skunky was nowhere near. "Stop!" he shouted, raising a hand.

"Stop? What do you mean, stop?" demanded Mr. Raccoon, still pulling away with all his might. "Have you forgotten how fast Dog can run?" He scowled at Chuck most disapprovingly.

"Dog hasn't been coming for some time," said Squirrel, who had left the procession from time to time to scamper up a tree and have a look. "Rabbit's got him sidetracked way over in the direction of the Next County."

Mr. Raccoon held up a silencing hand to test Squirrel's news. Those who could, turned and twisted their ears. Others cupped their hands behind their ears. It was true. Dog's barks were very distant and getting fainter.

"Still no reason to delay," Mr. Raccoon said. "Sidetracks sometimes lead back to the right tracks."

"But my point is that Skunky is no longer with us," said Chuck, pointing to the empty trap.

All eyes turned to the trap. All jaws went slack.

Squirrel, quite upset because he had had the best chance of all to observe what had been going on and missed it, began to chatter disconnectedly. "Skunky not in trap? Where? How? When? Did the end door come open? Will Dog get him? All of him—head—foot—tail—smell?"

"Hush, Squirrel," commanded Mrs. Raccoon, for all the little meadow mice had begun to whimper and cry. She, along with Mother 'Possum, stepped closer to the trap and began to look for clues. There was blood and a few black and white hairs, splintered wood, and twisted wire.

"It appears to me," said Beaver, who was quite knowledgeable in the ways of wood and lumber, "that somewhere along the line part of that trap came loose and slipped out, and Skunky with it."

"That being the case, we must forthwith retrace our steps and see what we can find," said Mr. Raccoon.

Solemnly the friends of the Grassy Meadow, Deep Forest, and Rustling Brook lined up two abreast behind Mr. Raccoon and headed back the way they had come.

"He was with us when we passed the maple grove," whispered Chipmunk to Chuck.

"He was still there when we went by Sassafras Gully," said Head Frog to D.P. "For I fell behind and came up out of the gully behind the trap. Even spoke to him. Said, 'How you doin', Skunky?' "

"What did he say?" asked D.P.

"Nothin'. Had no breath for it."

It was not difficult to find the way they had come. Grass was bent. Rocks were scratched. Old twigs were broken. When they came to the log where Skunky lay, half-hidden, everyone hopped right over and continued their worried, hurried, searching journey. Skunky, too weak to move or speak or even spray a little of his protective perfume to let them know where he was, heard them come and go, and a tear rolled from the corner of his eye and dropped onto the ground.

12
Rabbit Leads Dog Away

When Rabbit slipped out of his place in the tugging line, he told no one of his intentions. He wasn't sure that what he had in mind would work.

Straight down the fencerow he went, in the very direction of oncoming Dog, making no attempt to keep hidden, for his purpose was to be seen, smelled, and chased. He had been chased by Dog before and knew of many briar patches and woodpiles where he could find safety and time for breathing spells.

On and on he went, resolutely, into the face of danger in spite of the fearful beating of his heart. Dog was certainly very stupid today, he thought, or else very near-sighted. Not until Rabbit was within ten feet of him and had made an exceedingly high jump, a really grandstand play, did Dog see.

Dog swerved to right angles, let out a rapid series of excited barks, and unknowingly fell into Rabbit's "trap", which was much more sophisticated than any wooden-ended, wire box with a trap door. For it was Rabbit's plan to lead Dog far enough away to give Skunky's friends time to free him.

Round the fence corner Rabbit bounded. Across the hay field, past the cedar grove, through a rail fence. Dog was right behind, too close for comfort. Rabbit had to find a resting place sooner than he thought, for the pulling and tugging he'd done to try to help free Skunky had got him off to a breathless start. He headed for a place where the brambles were especially thick. Here he rested while Dog ran around, baffled and exasperated.

Just when it appeared that Dog was getting uninterested, Rabbit popped out of the briar patch, practically under the nose of Dog, and they were off again.

For over an hour Rabbit circled around in familiar haunts, returning from time to time to the briar patch for a brief rest. Now he felt it was time to make one last run, to lead Dog way off. Surely by this time Skunky had been set free or been taken away in some manner to safety. Mentally, Rabbit sifted through his points of safety and decided on a woodpile he knew of way over by the distant woods. There he'd stay for a long rest and nap until Dog grew weary and gave up. Then he'd find a clover patch, have supper, and make his way back home. There would be some kind of celebration for Skunky's rescue. Games, good food, good talk.

Rabbit sighed with deep satisfaction that he had such friends as those of the Grassy Meadow, Deep Forest, and Rustling Brook. Every one of them, the way they were working to free Skunky, were worthy of the Deep Forest Award. He did a few stretching exercises, took a deep breath, and emerged from the briar thicket where Dog would be sure to see.

He was not twenty feet from his hiding place, Dog on his tracks, when "Bang" went a barking stick. A quick searing pain stabbed Rabbit's left thigh. He somersaulted in midair and landed in a position facing the oncoming Dog. Despite the pain, he reversed himself, but knew that he had lost time and would have to run faster than he had ever run in his life. "Bang! Bang!" went the barking stick again. Rabbit heard pellets drop around him, but felt no further stinging pain. Each time his feet touched the ground, he felt the hot breath of Dog on his heels. The close barking was raucous in his ears and most distracting.

After a half mile of running in a straight direction, Rabbit knew that he was making no headway. He had not gained an inch on Dog, and the pain in his thigh was beginning to get worse. He noticed that when he leaped, he tended to land a little to the left of where he should. A fraction of a second was lost in balancing for the next leap. This would never do. Ten seconds lost and Dog's teeth would be clamping on his hind legs.

Knowing that because of his smaller body he could swerve to the right and left faster than Dog, he began to do that very thing. Zig, zag. Zig, zag. His forward progress toward the woodpile was slowed, but after awhile he saw that he was making some slight gain on Dog. It was not enough to allow him time to stop and get a good breath, though, and a good breath was what he needed now, very badly.

Past another cornfield, in and out of a gully, across a clearing, through a woods, went Rabbit. His sides heaved. His left leg was beginning to feel numb. His breath came in short painful gasps. Sadly he knew that he could not hold out much longer. Maybe this was to be the end of everything for him. And it was such a lovely day, with sunshine and shadow and fragrant little breezes. He thought of his friends and wished that he'd been able in his lifetime to have told them how much he loved them. Now, he supposed, it was going to be too late.

But wait! This was the last woods before the wood-pile he had been aiming for. If he could hold out just a little longer— He paused and allowed himself one good breath before plunging ahead. Just around that corner— "Come on feet—come on—come—" His eyes narrowed. His ears dropped. The left hind leg dragged uselessly, but now he was around the corner and—where was the woodpile? His heart sank lower than ever. The woodpile had been burned. There was nothing but a pile of soft ashes.

Not having time to think, to plot, to analyze what might be the best thing to do now, Rabbit simply plunged ahead. What ground he had gained was fast being lost, and he was now in unfamiliar territory. When he came to a log, there was no time to stop and inspect it to see if it had a hollow place where he might hide. What appeared to be a thicket might just be a tangle of weeds which Dog could easily penetrate. He resorted again to zig-zagging and gained a precious few seconds, time enough for him to judge the quicker route to a few scraggly trees ahead.

Each breath was now like a flame of fire flaring up in his chest. He felt dizzy and faint and was just about to drop in his tracks when a short distance ahead he saw a raccoon. Flying past he called, "Help me!" but dared not stop, so did not hear the grumpy reply, "Help yourself, Bub."

Slower and slower grew Rabbit's pace. Faster and

faster came Dog. A few feet ahead was a thicket Rabbit would just have to take a chance on. With one last valiant effort he pulled his aching body forward, squeezed in among some scratchy briars, interweaving vines, and rusty wire, and collapsed.

The clamping jaws of Dog came down, but all they closed on was a few hairs of Rabbit's tail and some rusty wire which hurt his mouth. He gave a short yap of pain, a few desultory barks, then, as if tiring of the whole adventure, turned and started home.

Rabbit did not know that he had escaped, for he lay motionless in a faint. Neither did he know that he was now in the Next County.

13
Rabbit and Little Mocker Meet in the Next County

Little Mocker, from his perch in the very thicket where Rabbit lay, had seen Rabbit's desperate struggle to escape from Dog and was pleased, although he did not recognize Rabbit as the rabbit he had known in the Grassy Meadow. His life here in this Next County had not been easy. There were times when he was so weak from lack of food that he could barely make it to the ground to look for seeds. But then, miraculously, the briars around him began to grow berries that turned red, then black, and had a sweet flavour. He could eat all he wanted without making the difficult and fearful trip to the ground. Thus he gained strength and courage, and after a few weeks began to range a little farther.

Although he had tried to make friends, it was seemingly impossible. There was something missing here. He didn't know what it was and spent many hours trying to figure it out, asking himself such questions as, "Why does everyone seem so angry? Why do they not try to help each other? Why do they not have neat, well-kept homes where others are welcome? Why is there such a difference between this place and the Grassy Meadow? Why? Why? Why?"

Could it be that the Keeper was not here? Oh, no, no. He quickly crossed out that question. Mrs. Raccoon said He was everywhere, and Little Mocker believed it.

Wasn't He there to put him on the plank in the river? And who else could make the new berries come? Plus a whole lot of other things Little Mocker could think of. But the other questions made him dizzy, and lack of answers left him unhappy and unsettled.

Sometimes when Little Mocker remembered Mrs. Raccoon and Skunky and Chuck and all the others, he grew so homesick a great ache would spread over his whole body. He supposed he would never see them again. At such times he would put his head beneath his wing and cry.

There were times when he thought he had made a friend. One morning, not long after he had come to the thicket, he heard a new song. Looking around for its source, he saw a bright yellow bird.

"That was beautiful," he complimented the bird when the song was finished.

"Thank you," came a most friendly reply. "Do you sing?"

"Some," said Little Mocker. "Is this your home?"

"Oh, no. Just passing through. It's the migration, you know."

"The what?" asked Little Mocker.

"The migration. Don't you migrate?"

Little Mocker did not know the word and felt it a great kindness of the yellow bird to go on and explain without ridiculing his ignorance. "Some of us fly north in summertime and then back south when cold weather comes. I'm headed north for a while."

And that was the way it had been, bird after bird. However, Little Mocker had gained from their passing flights. From each he had learned a new song. Sometimes at midnight when he couldn't sleep he'd practise them, putting together random phrases, making new and different arrangements until his were the sweetest songs ever sung in the Next County. Mostly his songs

98

spoke of the little breezes bending the dew-sparkly grass, of cozy little homes, friendship, laughter, daisies in old fence corners, silver slanting rain, pink pearly dawns. But interlaced with these bursts of melodious joy would be minor notes speaking of the fear, despair, and sorrow he had come to know.

The hauntingly beautiful music disturbed the residents. After a particularly beautiful song that seemed to pluck some long forgotten string deep and hidden inside them, they would be silent for a moment and thoughtful. Soon, however, they would recover their ill temper and shout insults such as, "Why don't you shut up, Noisy?" "Get lost." "When you leaving, Rowdy? Today? Huh? Huh? Today?"

For a while thereafter, maybe several days and nights, Little Mocker would be silent, for he was in no position to escape from their wrath should they decide to do something violent. From his perch in the tangled thicket, he was fairly safe from most of the mean and angry residents, but there were some who could climb and squeeze into the tightest of places.

Now, as he looked down on the helpless rabbit, Little Mocker felt a great kinship with him. He knew that no one in these parts would stop to help. In fact, the rabbit probably would be kicked in the side if the mean and mangy raccoon who roamed the muddy riverbanks happened to want to walk that way. Worse still, the rabbit might be mauled and cuffed and scratched to death by unseen creatures in the night and tomorrow eaten by crows.

Little Mocker thought of the time when he had lain helpless after the fall of the great hickory and of how Mrs. Raccoon of the Grassy Meadow had cared for him, set his wing, gave him hope, told him of the Keeper of All Creatures, and brought him back to health. Such thoughts were very pleasant. He sang a soft little song in praise of people who helped other people in their distress. Then, with a start, he stopped his song in the middle of a phrase and berated himself for sitting there singing when he could be helping. He didn't know exactly what he could do, but he began to descend in his awkward, fluttering, one-winged way to where the rabbit lay.

"Hello," he said. But there was no response, only laboured breathing. With his good wing, Little Mocker brushed dirt from the rabbit's nose. Then he picked pieces of weeds and briars from his fur, noticing there was blood oozing from his hind leg. "Hello," he said again and noticed this time there was a slight twitching of the rabbit's ears as if he had heard.

Little Mocker decided there was nothing to do, but just stay close until the rabbit could recover enough to tell him what to do. Remembering how Mrs. Raccoon had stayed close to him in his distress and spoke in such reassuring tones, Little Mocker did likewise. "You're going to be all right, rabbit. I'll be a friend. And there is nothing better in the whole world than a friend."

It was late in the afternoon before Rabbit opened his eyes.

"Hello," Little Mocker tried again.

This time Rabbit responded. "Hello," he said, but it was barely audible.

More hours passed during which Little Mocker sang little snatches of songs, fanned Rabbit with his good wing, and kept the flies away.

By sundown Rabbit again opened his eyes and tried to sit up, but it was more of a hunched-up leaning against the brambles. "Where am I?" he asked.

Little Mocker's heart leaped joyously. Perhaps here was someone from outside this terrible Next County. "Is this new territory to you?" he asked.

Rabbit looked around, stretching his neck as best he could so as to see what lay beyond this fencerow thicket. "I've never been here before in all my life. I am quite lost. You see I was chased by—" He stopped in midsentence, remembering Dog, and began to shiver.

"It's all right," Little Mocker assured. "Dog is gone. But—"

"But what?" asked Rabbit, sensing that all was not well.

"Well, there are others here."

"Other dogs?"

"No. Not exactly."

"Not exactly? What do you mean?"

Little Mocker was reluctant to tell the strange rabbit that he had wandered into bad territory, especially since it appeared that, like himself, it might be some time before he could get away again.

"What do you mean, not exactly other dogs?" Rabbit insisted.

"Other creatures."

"Like what?"

"Oh, there's a raccoon lives here and—"

"Raccoon?" Rabbit interrupted. "Raccoons aren't anything to be afraid of. I know a raccoon where I come from that is one of the nicest friends I have."

Again Little Mocker's heart leaped joyously. He looked at the rabbit intensely, studying the whiskers, the big eyes, the lift of the eyebrows, the brown of the fur. Then the questions came tumbling out. "Did the raccoon have seven rings in her tail? Did she have a neat little home in a hollow tree at the edge of a place called the Grassy Meadow?"

Noticing that the rabbit's eyes were growing larger and brighter with each question, Little Mocker burst out, "Are you Rabbit from Grassy Meadow?"

At this Rabbit sat up on his hind feet, painful

though it was, and extended a hand in greeting. "I am that rabbit," he said. "Have I met you before?"

"Rabbit! I am Little Mocker!"

"Little Mocker!" Rabbit exclaimed. He had to lie back down. "Little Mocker," he repeated. "Are you sure?" he asked, and laughed feebly at his own question. "Of course you are, it's just that, that—you've changed."

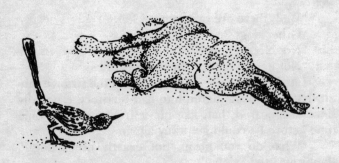

"Oh, yes, I've changed," Little Mocker admitted. "A scraggly looking sight I am with these wing feathers broken and poor and skinny and when I fly—well, really I can't fly. I just flutter and hop and scoot."

"Oh, I didn't mean that," Rabbit hastened to say, fearing he had hurt Little Mocker's feelings. "You had spots on your breast and were more brown than this grey."

"Oh that," said Little Mocker. "Those were my baby spots. My mother told me they would go away and that I'd get these white bars across my wings and tail." He spread his good wing and his tail feathers to show Rabbit his new colouring.

"Very handsome," Rabbit complimented. "Tell me, did you find your mother?"

"No," replied Little Mocker sadly.

"But you must have. You have learned to sing. I

heard you even when I was so faint I couldn't move. I think I might have died if I hadn't held on to those wonderful songs. I told myself, 'Rabbit, now you just hold on—hold on—hold on to those beautiful songs. As long as you hold on to those songs, you'll live. I think if you had stopped, I'd have been done in, and I thank you." He lowered his eyes and said, more softly, "You know, for a while I thought it must be the Keeper singing."

Little Mocker did not reply readily. He was deeply touched by what Rabbit had just said. But in all the time he had been copying the songs of the other birds that lived here or passed through on their great northern migrations, he felt that he was doing something wrong, "rippin' 'em right out of the air," as the strange Next County bird had advised. Tears welled up in his eyes, and he flung his head sharply to get rid of them.

"Yes, I learned to sing," he admitted. He thought of asking Rabbit's opinion of the manner in which he had learned to sing. But it being such a serious subject to him and Rabbit still very sick, he turned the conversation to other things, asking about Mr. and Mrs. Raccoon, Mother 'Possum, Squirrel, Chuck, Skunky, and all the rest.

"They were all just fine this morning. I guess it was this morning. How long have I been here?" Rabbit asked.

"Yes, it was this morning you squeezed through the fence and into these brambles just in time."

"They were all just fine, except Skunky maybe."

"Finally fell down and broke a rib?" asked Little Mocker, remembering Skunky's love of demonstrating the fall of the old hickory.

"No. Skunky got caught in a trap. A trap that was really meant for me. I knew where it was and forgot to tell the others."

"Did he get out?"

"I'm not sure. Oh, he must have by now. But I'm really not sure."

"You didn't stay to see?" asked Little Mocker.

"Well, you see, Dog was coming. Everybody was there, and I can run faster than Dog—"

"So you led Dog away," interrupted Little Mocker. "That was a wonderful thing to do, Rabbit. They don't do things like that here."

"Here? Where is here?"

Before Little Mocker had a chance to answer, he heard the snarls, squalls, meows, and hisses of the creature he had heard the night of his blindness. For a moment he was rigid with fear, remembering the quick, stabbing pain of sharp teeth in his neck. Then, "Quick, Rabbit. Crawl in as far as you can under those rocks and briars. Don't let one hair stick out!"

Then, flitting and fluttering in his one-winged way, Little Mocker made it from branch to branch until he was ten or twelve feet above the ground. He hopped carefully out to a small branch which he had learned could not hold the weight of any menacing Next County creature. When he felt he was safe, he stopped to look down to see if Rabbit was safe. Not seeing one hair of him, he turned his attention to the creature that was bounding through the tall weeds.

14
Little Mocker Seeks Help for Rabbit

Had it not been for the tightly drawn lips exposing sharp teeth and a most unfriendly look in the eyes, Little Mocker would have thought the creature quite handsome. It had short sleek hair, a stubby tail, and yellowish sides, spotted and streaked with black. There was a tuft of hair on each cheek and smaller tufts at the end of peaked, upright ears.

For a moment, Little Mocker thought it was going on by, but then it stopped short, sniffed the air, and turned in the direction of the very pile of rocks and briars where Rabbit was hidden. The snarls and hisses increased, and sharp claws came out of big furry paws to scratch at the weeds and rocks.

Little Mocker trembled with fear for Rabbit, but he began to sing. It was the only thing he knew to do. If it did not divert the snarling creature's attention, perhaps it would calm Rabbit's fear.

For over an hour the strange creature clawed and scratched at Rabbit's hiding place. He would dislodge some rocks, sniff, lie down in quietness, get up, dislodge more rocks. Finally he walked away, still growling and snarling. When he was out of sight, Little Mocker descended to Rabbit's hiding place and called out, "Rabbit? Are you all right?"

"No," came the faint reply. "A rock has fallen on me, and I can't move."

A tremor of despair passed over Little Mocker. He knew that he could not move the rocks, and where in all this Next County would he find someone to help? However, he said as cheerfully as he could, "Never mind, Rabbit, I'll get some help."

Without hesitation, Little Mocker began hopping, flitting, and fluttering in the direction of the muddy river. During long hot summer days when he had grown weary of his thicket hideout, he had made his rickety way to the top of the tall elm where he could see far in all directions. He came to know that at some time during the day all those who lived in this dreary place went to the river to drink.

He met the meadow mice first, probably the same two he had first encountered in this place, he thought, for they were as unfriendly as ever, sticking their noses in the air and prancing right on by as if they hadn't heard his urgent request for help.

When he saw the raccoon approaching, little sharp stabs of fear danced up and down his spine. Nevertheless, he stopped right in front of the raccoon and said, "Sir, I have a friend in trouble. Will you come and lift a rock off him?"

"Who? Me? Lifting rocks? Get out of my way, pipsqueak." He took a swipe at Little Mocker. But being a bit more wary this time, Little Mocker was able to hop backward far enough to escape the force of the blow.

Up and down the riverbank, Little Mocker went. In response to his pleas for help, the river rat said, "Help? What's that?" His expression was so sincere that Little Mocker actually thought he didn't know what the word meant, and started to explain, whereupon the river rat plunged into the river, calling back over his shoulder, "Help doesn't grow in these parts. It's every one for himself."

Not one would help. "And just to lift a rock," Little Mocker muttered to himself. Wearily he returned to where Rabbit lay buried beneath the rocks, but he did not have the heart to tell him of his failure. "You all right, Rabbit?" he asked.

"All right," Rabbit replied, although he too was being more cheerful than he felt, for the rocks were hurting his leg.

"We'll be helping you soon," Little Mocker said. He hadn't the slightest idea what to do next, and it was getting dark, but he felt that he must keep up Rabbit's spirits.

He fluttered around in his usual circles, trying to get off the ground. Oh, to fly again, to fly to somewhere beyond this place and get help! His brain went around in circles even faster than his body until he was quite exhausted. And as always, when exhausted he thought of the comfort he had once known wrapped in Mrs. Raccoon's Flower Garden quilt and the kindness of all those former friends. When his mind got around to Mr. Raccoon and his managerial qualities, Little Mocker made his plans. "Now what I'll have to do," he said, "is, dark or no dark, start out in the direction from which I saw Rabbit come, and maybe eventually I'll find someone who will help."

Having come to this conclusion, Little Mocker started out in his slow and awkward way. He noted well the tall elm which he had often laboriously ascended to observe the countryside. Towering far above other trees, he felt that if he could always keep it in sight he wouldn't get lost.

It was frightening thrashing along on the ground after dark. Progress was very, very slow. At one point, fearing he would become hopelessly lost, he waited and waited for the moon to come up. When he could see the tall elm outlined against the sky, he continued.

Crickets, beetles, and assorted night-noisy bugs ceased their sound when they heard Little Mocker approaching. He wished they wouldn't, for he felt that it would help to cover the noise he made himself as he hopped along through dry grasses, rustling leaves, old cornstalks, and other raspy underfoot things. At times he grew so terribly tired he had to stop and rest. Other times he was so convinced that he ought to be back near Rabbit, singing encouraging little songs, that he actually backtracked. Then, overcome by better judgment, he turned again and plunged onward.

At sunrise, looking back at the big elm, he supposed he hadn't come half a mile, which was most discouraging. But now that the darkness was over, maybe he'd encounter someone he might ask for help.

Sixteen large geese flew over, but he couldn't get their attention. Anyway, he didn't suppose they'd have any way of combining their strength enough to move a pile of rocks. He met two baby toads or frogs—he didn't know which—who hopped away in great haste. "Must have thought I was going to eat them," Little Mocker mumbled unhappily.

As he stood watching the disappearing toads or frogs, he noticed, out of the corner of his eye, a strange movement in the ground. It seemed to push upward in a crumbly fashion as if some unseen, underground plough were at work. And it was coming right toward him, the soil rising higher and higher, stopping, starting, stopping, starting.

Little Mocker stood quite still, not knowing what to make of this strange affair. Then, all at once, right in front of him, a very sharp pointed little nose thrust through the ground, followed by a head with two of the tiniest ears Little Mocker had ever seen and the silkiest fur.

"Good morning," Little Mocker greeted in a cheery voice, although he was trembling with fear at this creature which appeared to have no eyes at all, a short round body, and enormous forelegs with long broad toenails that looked as if they could rip a person to death with one swipe.

"It's a fine morning," Little Mocker continued as if he were quite willing to spend a pleasant hour chatting about the beauties of the countryside. "I don't believe we've met."

"Oh, I'm Mole," said the silky looking creature, looking around to see where this voice might be coming from. "Beg your pardon, but I don't see very well," he apologized.

"Do you have no eyes?" asked Little Mocker, wondering immediately if he should have asked such a personal question.

"Oh, yes," replied Mole, lifting up some overhanging fur with his broad toenails to reveal two pinpoint sized eyes. "But you see, I don't need sight very much where I live."

"And where is that?" Little Mocker asked.

"Anywhere underground that I choose."

"Underground!" exclaimed Little Mocker.

"Oh, it is very pleasant underground," assured Mole. "Never too cold. Never too hot. Plenty of food. No glare. No signs saying, 'Keep off the grass,' 'No trespassing.' Very, very cozy. Where do you live?"

"Me? I live in fencerows and shrubs and trees and in the air—that is, I fly through the air from place to place, or rather did at one time. Due to an unfortunate accident, I suppose I will never fly again. I just hop and scrabble around now in a very slow fashion. In fact, see that elm tree over yonder?"

Mole lifted the fur from his eye in an attempt to see, but said, "No, I don't see anything. What is a tree?"

Looking at the landmark, Little Mocker suddenly remembered why he was this far away from it and began immediately to tell Mole of the plight of Rabbit and that he was looking for someone who could help.

"Hmmmm," said Mole. And then again, "Hmmmm." And then, not being able to see for himself, he asked, "How far is it to your elm tree?"

"About half a mile."

"Well, I think I'm your man!" exclaimed Mole.

"You? Oh, Mole, can you lift rocks?" Little Mocker asked, his heart leaping with joy.

"No, not exactly lift. But I can burrow down under where Rabbit is, loosen the earth, and make a tunnel for him to come up out of."

Such a gladness suffused Little Mocker's body that he felt he could fly straight up into the air as far as he wanted to go. In fact, the feeling was so powerful that he tried it. Of course, he was able to lift himself only a few feet, but in doing so a strange thing happened—one of the broken wing feathers fell out and drifted to the ground. His joy in being able to help Rabbit kept him from paying much attention to it, only to note, upon alighting again, that he felt better without it, and thought he probably presented a better appearance with one of the dragging, frazzly things gone.

"Well, let's go!" Little Mocker said without further delay. "Can you travel up here with me, or do you have to go underground?"

"I can travel both ways. I have very good hearing, so could follow you even if I traveled underground, but since this air does smell fresh this morning, I'll just follow you. Lead on!"

"I must tell you that there are unfriendly creatures around here that like to fight," Little Mocker said. He could hardly get the words out, but felt it only fair to warn Mole. He had no more than finished his sentence when Mole disappeared right before Little Mocker's eyes, and the only sign left was a little spot of churned-up earth.

"What have I done?" Little Mocker berated himself. "Here I had some help for Rabbit and scared him out of it." But no sooner had he finished the thought when, right in front of him, up came the little sharp pointed nose followed by the rest of the silky body.

"Oh," sighed Little Mocker. "I thought you were gone for good."

"Just a demonstration," said Mole.

Knowing how long he had been gone, and how heavy the rocks had been on Rabbit, and how weak he was, Little Mocker began to tremble with fear as they approached the pile of rocks. Maybe they were too late.

"This is it," Little Mocker told Mole when they were close. He put his head near the rocks and called, "Rabbit, are you still there?"

Back came the faintest of sounds, but it was enough to give Little Mocker great hope.

"Now, just about right here, Mole, is where Rabbit

is trapped," Little Mocker instructed, seeing to it that Mole was close enough to know where to start his tunnel.

Mole immediately disappeared again, leaving a little pile of churned-up earth.

"Rabbit," Little Mocker continued, "help is coming. A mole is going to make a tunnel for you. Be feeling for some loosened earth beneath you, and try to come on up and out." He then began to sing a song that sounded like, "Cheer-up, cheer-up," which he had, in the past, heard some bird singing and thought was a very good thing to sing right now.

In fact, Little Mocker felt pretty cheerful himself this morning, having met someone who was kind and willing to help. And Rabbit was still alive. And one of his frazzly feathers was gone. He spread his wings as he remembered this, and then, of all things, he saw a long feather from his good wing fall out. This might have lowered his spirits some if at that very moment he hadn't felt the earth loosening right beneath where he stood. He hopped aside, and there was Mole's funny little nose coming up out of the ground. Soon his whole body was glistening in the morning sun. In a few minutes here came Rabbit, who wasn't able to come up through Mole's tunnel, but, finding the ground beneath him loosened enough, was able to scrabble and scratch his way to freedom.

The first thing Little Mocker noticed was that Rabbit's wound seemed better. "It actually looks better, Rabbit," Little Mocker exclaimed.

"It has been lying next to the good earth," Mole said, "and the good earth is a great healer. It's just like a sponge, soaking up so many of our hurts and the things we don't want and then giving back in return food and a place to live."

No telling how long Mole might have gone on in

praise of earth if Little Mocker hadn't noticed that now blood was coming from one of Mole's front toes. "Oh, Mole. You've hurt yourself."

Mole looked down at his toe. "Well, so I have. Looks as if I've broken off a claw. I came up against a rock down there unexpectedly. But think nothing of it. It will grow back, and I can still dig." To prove it, he did his famous disappearing act, only to reappear When he had breathed enough fresh air to gain strength, Rabbit began to try to express his thanks, but Mole and Little Mocker made him hush and said the thing he needed now was food and water. "Which reminds me, I'm pretty hungry myself," said Mole, who then, with a cheery "See you around sometime," disappeared. This time Little Mocker and Rabbit decided it was for good. They waited and waited for him to reappear. When he didn't, they began to sing the Grassy Meadow farewell song, "Farewell, Little Mole, Farewell," and so forth. Then they, too, began to look around for some food.

15

D.P. and Friends Retrieve the Brass Cornered Box

Although things were beginning to look brighter for Rabbit and Little Mocker, back at the hickory stump beside the Grassy Meadow their friends were very despondent. There were sighs and wrinkled brows and much nervous twitchings and twaddlings. Occasionally, seeing some motion in the grass which indicated that someone was approaching, faces would brighten expectantly. But so far it had always turned out to be someone returning from a scouting trip to see what could be learned about Skunky or Rabbit.

It had been more than twenty-four hours since Skunky had been discovered missing from the trap, and the only reports that had come trickling in were that Rabbit was certainly not at his home, hadn't been there all night, for Chipmunk had stayed in Rabbit's burrow for the very purpose of finding out if he had come home. The same went for Skunky. No piece of whisker, ear, or tail, or toenail could be found.

Mr. and Mrs. Raccoon, Mother 'Possum, D.P., and Chuck had prowled the woods all through the night in the hope of finding some sign of either one.

Various blue jays reported they had seen Dog back at his home, but of course they couldn't tell from looking at Dog whether he'd done in either of their friends.

Wearily the hours ticked by. Everyone who had

been out hunting returned to sit in a sad, silent circle. Finally Mr. Raccoon said, "Now what we'll have to do is stop this gloomy sitting around waiting for scouts to come back one at a time. Let's all get our food and rest, but keep constantly on the lookout, spending our spare moments looking anywhere and everywhere. Leave no log unturned, no pile of leaves intact. Then we'll all meet back here at morning, noon, and sundown for updated reports of territory covered."

It seemed the best thing to do. So all departed, heavy-hearted but still full of determination.

Mrs. Raccoon climbed to her neat little home, where she spoke fervently to the Keeper about the safety of both Skunky and Rabbit. Then she cleaned everything in sight, although it was already spotlessly clean.

Mother 'Possum happened to think of a hollow log she hadn't visited in a long time. It could be that Skunky, and maybe Rabbit too, had crawled into it and couldn't get out.

D.P. started toward his dump pile, thinking what a stupendous task it would be to explore all the nooks and crannies of that edifice. He was trying to outline a plan in his mind of where he might start when he tripped and fell over something. Turning to see what it was, he noted a length of binder twine. At first he was very cross about it and muttered darkly, "Drat and bosh and flumm-drummit." Then he realized it was the very piece of twine he had put there himself to guide his future helpers toward the bright coloured box inside the dump. It seemed weeks ago since he had left that marker there. But really it was only some time yesterday. Having no better plan of where to start looking in his castle in the far-fetched hope of finding Skunky or Rabbit, he followed the binder twine trail back to the brightly painted box, slumped against it, and went to sleep.

D.P. slept until long after daylight. Might have slept all day, he was so tired, but a sudden jarring from one of his upper storeys woke him. It made one of the lights inside the box come on. He looked at it for some time, expecting it to go out, but it didn't. In fact, it provided enough illumination for D.P. to see the lettering on the side of the box. He wished to goodness he could read. Suddenly he remembered that Head Frog must be able to read since he could spell even some of the biggest kinds of words, like *resuscitation.*

He was of a mind to go and get Head Frog right away, but then there seemed to be something else more important he needed to do. He shook his head vigorously as if to shed all remnants of sleep and stir his brain to alertness.

It worked, for immediately he remembered that Skunky and Rabbit were lost and everyone needed to do something about it. Quickly he sought out his emergency pantry where he kept things for quick meals. Then, still chewing on some sharp cheese, he emerged from his home and hurried to the hickory stump meeting-place to learn if there had been any overnight developments.

"Not a thing," reported Chipmunk who had agreed to stay at the stump as a sort of anchorman while all others pursued the hunt.

"We all met here at sunrise as planned," continued Chipmunk, giving D.P. a reproving look.

"I know. I know, Chip," D.P. said, hanging his head in shame. "The simple fact is that I didn't wake up."

"We're all tired, D.P., but we must press on."

"Yes, we must," D.P. readily agreed, already making plans of how he might secure help for exploring his huge home. "I need the meadow mice," he said. "And perhaps the frogs. Anyone small enough to crawl

117

around in my hallways without making the whole thing tumble down. It just could be that Skunky and Rabbit, knowing what a good hiding place it is, squeezed in somewhere and can't get out."

Chipmunk shaded his eyes against the glare of the morning sun and turned in a slow circle to see if he could see anyone coming, possibly with good news. "We're all to meet here again at noon. Remember? You can make your requests then."

Never had the Grassy Meadow, Deep Forest, and Rustling Brook territory had such a thorough searching. Grass was bent low, logs turned over; a multitude of tracks decorated the edges of the streams. Overhead jays, swallows, warblers, wagtails, thrushes, and all manner of feathered friends scanned the countryside.

The noon meeting came with no good report. D.P. asked for the help he needed and got it.

"We's will find him if he's in the dump," chorused all the meadow mice as they moved along toward D.P's home. The frogs winked and blinked. All except Head Frog, who was explaining to D.P. that he feared his family would not be too good at this. "If some of the hallways are not very high overhead, the manner in which we ambulate—"

"Whoa!" said D.P. "What's ambulate?"

"A-M-B-U-L-A-T-E," spelled Head Frog, "meaning the way we get around. We're likely to bump our heads on your ceilings and—ah—mess things up a bit."

D.P. was about to reply that it wouldn't hurt his ceilings or Frog's head, whichever Frog was talking about, when it came to him that Head Frog had just spelled another big word, which proved again that he must be able to read. D.P. twitched his whiskers, whipped his tail, and urged the whole crew to hurry up.

When they arrived at the dump pile, D.P. quickly

divided his work crew into four squadrons and marked off areas for them to search. "Now don't be afraid," he cautioned. "Things might shift once in a while. My walls aren't exactly stationary. You can always get back out, small as you are. Just start at the bottom and keep working up, and when you come out on top, wait for everyone else so no one will come up missing. You all know up from down, don't you?"

"Yes, sir," said the mice. "We's not afraid." They immediately disappeared into the many openings.

The little frogs said nothing and sat all in a row.

"Now, it's all right," Head Frog assured them. "I know it is not a place where you like to go, but there are times when we have to do things we don't especially like."

At this, the little frogs edged forward and cautiously disappeared into the dump.

"Head Frog, you come with me," said D.P. He found his trail of twine and soon had Head Frog standing before the brass cornered box which, much to D.P.'s surprise, now had three lights burning. "See this lettering here on the side of this thing? What does it say?"

Head Frog hopped as close as he could and began to read. " 'When all buttons are pushed and all lights burning, ask any question of me and I will have the answer.' Amazing," he said, and then again, "Amazing. D.P., what times we live in!" He hopped all around and over the box. "And here on this side it says, 'Little Toy Computer, Mfg., Dayton, Ohio, pat. pend.' Amazing!" He gave D.P. a curious look. "Why have you kept this from us, D.P.? Here we could have had the answer to where Rabbit and Skunky are all the time."

"Well, you see—" D.P. hung his head. "I can't read."

"Oh, yes. Yes, of course. Well, no matter. Let's

push the buttons, light the lights, and ask where we can find Skunky and Rabbit."

"That's another thing," D.P. explained. "They don't all light up, and the only thing I've ever heard it say is "Lo-lo-lo."

The two friends sat in silence for a while contemplating the marvels of the modern world and how to cope with them. Then Head Frog asked, "What's on the bottom?"

"Well, that I don't know," D.P. said. "I tried to move it, turn it over, but couldn't."

"We need to get it out of this place," Head Frog said as if talking to himself. Then, feeling that he might have hurt D.P.'s feelings by making such a remark about his home, he quickly apologized. "It's just that I can't see too well in here. And there might be some further instructions on the bottom."

D.P. brightened. "Well, you see, I've thought of that. You may have noticed that we followed a piece of binder twine in here. See, here's a bunch of it left. If we could tie it securely around this, this—what did you say it was?"

"Computer. C-O-M-P-U-T-E-R. Little Toy Computer."

"Computer," said D.P., glad to learn the name of the thing. "If we could tie it with rope, take the end of the rope outside, which I've already done, round up enough of us to pull it out, we might get at it better."

"Splendid!" shouted Head Frog so loud it jarred a nearby rusty colander, which in turn jarred a split baseball bat, which in turn jarred the computer. It began to say, "Lo-lo-lo-lo."

"Remarkable!" exclaimed Head Frog in a more hushed tone. "Let's get at this, D.P." He began to unwind a length of what was left of the binder twine.

Taking an end of it in his mouth, he jumped on top of the computer, bumping his head on a tangle of thin wire, then hopped down the other side. He landed in a three-pound coffee can. It took considerable effort to get out. D.P. came around to lend words of encouragement.

When he succeeded in getting out, Head Frog stopped to consider where the twine should go next. He scratched his head and winked and blinked. "It is apparent, D.P., that the twine needs to go underneath and back up the other side, tied on top, then down another side, underneath, and back on top again, and so forth. The problem is how to get underneath it."

"No problem at all, Head Frog," said D.P., transferring the twine to his own mouth and plunging in amongst the miscellaneous mound of stuff beneath the computer.

"Watch out, D.P.," shouted Head Frog, fearing that the computer and mountainous accumulation on top would crush the life out of his friend.

In no time at all, D.P. emerged on the other side of the computer and called for Head Frog to come around and see. They shook hands solemnly, looked wise, and probably would have laughed uproariously at what they had executed had they not feared the dump pile would come crashing down.

After that, the two friends combined their know-how efforts to secure the brightly painted box. Up and over and around they went, tying overhand knots, figure eight knots, cat's paw, fisherman's bend, clove, square, granny, and lark's head knots until the whole thing appeared as if it were enclosed in a binder-twine net.

"Now then," said D.P., dusting his hands and leaning back to look at what they had accomplished.

"Now then," repeated Head Frog, with the same sense of achievement. In a few minutes he asked, "Now then, what?"

"It is my plan," said D.P., speaking very slowly as if making up his mind as he talked. "Yes, it is my plan to follow the trail of binder twine to the outside, and then—and then—when all the meadow mice and lesser frogs gather at the top, we'll pull the thing out." His beady eyes brightened. He tweaked his whiskers and repeated very assuredly, "Yes sir, we'll pull the thing out and have a good look at it."

"Good thinking," complimented Head Frog.

Around broken table legs, twisted lampshades, and dented dishpans they went, taking time to look into jars and cans and likely looking places where Skunky or Rabbit might be.

When they emerged into the bright daylight, D.P. scampered to the top of the dump to see if there was any news from the searchers.

"We searched up and down and sideways and catty-cornered, and found no hide nor hair of Rabbit or Skunky," said Edward Meadow Mouse, reporting for the whole crew.

"We didn't neither," said one of the frogs.

"Are you all here?" asked D.P.

"Two frogs and Eileen, Hilda, Clara, Bernice, and Beth Meadow Mouses haven't come up yet," said Edward, who was keeping an acount on a piece of cardboard with the aid of a stub of chalk he had found.

"Hmmmm," said D.P., wondering to himself just what the pull power of two hundred and five meadow mice and twenty-five lesser frogs, one Head Frog, and himself might be.

"Mary Mouse," he said, looking out over the gathering, not being sure which one might be Mary, but being sure that there surely was one named Mary. "Come up here a minute."

A sleek little mouse moved up front, looking quite surprised that anyone had noticed her, special-like.

"Grab hold of my tail and pull," commanded D.P.

"Your tail? Grab hold? Oh, no sir, I couldn't," said Mary, beginning to back away. "We been taught not to pull anyone's tail. No, no, no, sir. That's bad manners. I can't do that."

"Yes, you can," D.P. said in a no-nonsense manner. "I haven't time to explain now, but it is important."

Hesitantly, blushing furiously, Mary Mouse took hold of D.P.'s tail and pulled. "Oh, sir, I don't like to do that at all," Mary apologized.

"It's all right," D.P. said, making himself as flexible as he could.

"Jimmy," D.P. called out, knowing there must be a Jimmy. "Grab hold and help Mary."

The two of them managed to move D.P. a fraction of an inch. When two more were added, Myrtle and Eulamae, they pulled D.P. easily.

"Good," exclaimed D.P. "Now, is everyone here?"

"They is all here, sir," said Edward. "But we don't understand this at all." Two hundred and thirty pairs of questioning, winking, blinking eyes were turned on D.P.

"You will." D.P. shook his head affirmatively. "Come, we have work to do."

Pell-mell they hopped, somersaulted, rolled, tumbled, and ran down the sides of the dump pile. Some thought maybe Skunky's or Rabbit's tail was visible somewhere, and they were going to pull them out by the tail. Others said that D.P. was going in after one of their friends in some upside-down place and they'd have to pull him back out by the tail.

By the time they all assembled at the foot of the dump, the wildest kinds of rumours had flashed through the crowd. "His tail is broken, and we's have got to set it," whispered Ulina Mouse.

"We's gonna drag him around and around over the Grassy Meadow, Deep Forest, and along the Rustling Brook so if anyone is harming Skunky or Rabbit, they'll smell a rat and go away," Stella Mouse told those around her.

"Silly Stella, that's not what 'smell a rat' means," chided Med Mouse.

"Well, I bet they would go away if they saw such a sight," said Elizabeth Mouse, coming to the aid of her friend Stella.

"Now listen to this," said D.P. He had climbed onto an oil drum where he could be heard better. "We have an object inside the dump we wish to pull out. It may help us to find Skunky and Rabbit. There is a length of binder twine right here." He pointed to where the twine emerged from the dump. "The end of it is over there by that pile of rocks. I want everyone to line up along that twine, grab hold of it, and when I say, 'Pull,' you all pull."

"We's gonna get to pull this time," said Ida Mouse, remembering how she and her kin had had to stand by and only watch while the others pulled Skunky's trap loose. "I bet we's good pullers."

"I hope so," said D.P., running up and down the length of the twine to see that everyone was properly positioned. He put the frogs, including Head Frog, at the end of the line, knowing they had a habit of falling over backwards when standing up to pull on anything. "Now we're not to jerk," he instructed. "A jerk might break the line. Just a steady, slow pull."

There were many questions about what they were attempting to pull out, but neither Head Frog nor D.P. thought it wise to try to explain the Little Toy Computer. They didn't know enough about it themselves. "Just a box," they replied to all the numerous questions.

"We's gonna find Skunky and Rabbit with a box," went the message down the line, and not being very familiar with the searching abilities of a box, no one questioned further.

Hands tightened on the twine. Faces showed determination. Muscles twitched.

"All right, pull!" commanded D.P.

The twine grew taut. A small rumble was heard inside the dump.

"Pull!" shouted D.P. again.

125

The rumble grew louder. Things clashed and banged and gonged and clinked and clanked.

"We're doing it," D.P. shouted and called again, "Pull!"

"We's doin' it. We's doin' it," went the relayed words of encouragement down the line.

Soon things began to shift and move on the surface of the dump. A paste jar came tumbling down, followed by a barbecue grill, a *No Trespassing* sign, and a broken-sided birdcage.

"You're doing splendidly," D.P. yelled louder than ever so as to be heard over the noise. "Pull!"

Soon a brass corner of the computer was shining in the sunlight. Then another and another. Through the network of twine could be seen flashing lights.

"Here it comes," shouted D.P. "Hurrah. You did it!" He lifted his clasped hands above his head in a gesture of triumph and congratulations.

The pullers laid down the twine, danced little jigs of victory, and ran around rejoicing, hugging, and complimenting each other. It wasn't often they were called upon to do anything important.

D.P. lifted a hand for silence. "This is a Little Toy Computer," he told them.

"A what?" came back a chorus of questions.

"A Little Toy Computer. It says here on the side that it has the answer to everything."

Heads shook in wonderment and disbelief. How could such a thing that didn't even have hair, whiskers, or skin have answers to everything? Giggles were heard here and there, but were hurriedly squelched as D.P. scanned the assembly with scolding eyes.

"When all these buttons are pushed and all the lights are flashing, we ask a question and get the answer," he explained.

"Push the buttons. Light the lights," two or three mice shouted. The words were instantly taken up by all the others, who got up to dance more little jigs and make a more sophisticated little song:

Flemmery, flammery, flum,
Out of the dump pile, box did come.
Push the buttons, light the lights,
Answers will come by day or night.

"Gellicky whiskers!" D.P. exclaimed, walking around the box. "This thing has come out upside down. Come here, Head Frog."

Head Frog hurriedly hopped closer, pulled apart some of the binder twine, and read further instructions. " 'Insert regular flashlight batteries inside this door.' " He looked at D.P. blankly and whispered, "What's a flashlight battery?"

"I'm not sure. But if we open the door maybe we'll find out," replied D.P.

"Brilliant thinking," Head Frog admitted, a little chagrined that he hadn't thought of it himself.

They went after the little door with tooth and toenail. They kicked it with their hind feet. D.P. whipped at it smartly with his tail, but the door would not give.

"What we'll have to do," sighed D.P. at last, "is get someone with stronger and more capable hands."

"Like Mrs. Raccoon," Head Frog suggested.

"Exactly," D.P. agreed rather loudly.

"Exactly," repeated all the little mice and frogs who had heard, and they added another couplet to their song:

> Flemmery, flammery, flum,
> Out of the dump pile, box did come.
> Push the buttons, light the lights,
> Answers will come by day or night.
> D.P. said it matter-of-factly,
> But he said it most exactly.

D.P. climbed on top of the computer for another announcement. "Due to unfortunate circumstances beyond our control, we are temporarily delayed in this project. I thank you for your services. When we get this thing to working, you will all have the privilege of using it. Ask a question, and out will come the answer."

They all started for the hickory stump, trying out their new composition to a variety of tunes.

16
Skunky Returns

During the days that followed Skunky's unconventional release from the trap, he lay under the log where he had been thrown, limp and helpless. He heard the searchers come and go, heard what some of them said, such as, "It won't be the same around here without old Skunky. He kept things livened up, he did, with his tree fallin' act. Always did it a different way, and each time made us believe that was the way it was."

Although he was too weak to call out or make his presence known in other ways, it pleased Skunky, even in his sickness, to think he had made life a little more pleasant for others. But the sad tone of their voices made it seem as if he were already gone. Many times he summoned every ounce of strength he could to try to scramble out where some part of him could be seen. But with all his bruises, scratches, soreness, and stiffened legs, all he succeeded in doing was getting himself further down in the loose soil and decayed leaves underneath the log.

One day it came to him that he was practically buried. Just the tip of his nose was exposed. The thought upset him so that it propelled words from his mouth: "Buried alive!" It was awful to hear them spoken aloud, just as if some judge were passing sentence. Besides, he got soil in his mouth which tasted terrible and served to remind him of how hungry he was.

After a little while, a more pleasant thought came to Skunky. If he could talk out loud, which he hadn't been able to do for some time, he must be getting stronger. He stretched his neck and was pleased to see that it brought his whole head out of the debris.

"Here I am!" he shouted, in case anyone might be near enough to hear him.

Skunky thought it was about the stillest place in the world. Not one blue jay called out from the tree-tops, nor a single mouse stirred so much as a spiderweb on the ground. Eventually he heard the distant drone of one of those huge sky butterflies that sounded a little like the trucks that came to the dump pile. But these sky creatures never landed, so far as Skunky or any of his friends knew. They just came into sight up in the air, over the line of trees bordering the Deep Forest, and disappeared into the blue. Others, the low flying kind, circled over the Grassy Meadow and seemed to disappear in the direction from which they came. Still others, distant cousins, they all felt, flew very high and left long white tracks behind them. Head Frog had been able to spell out, W-I-G-G-S C-R-O-P D-U-S-T—, on the low flying ones. But they always disappeared before he could get the whole message.

The sunshine filtering through the tree leaves felt good on his head, and little breezes brought Skunky the smell of the woodland floor, which was minty and served to clear his mind for some orderly thinking.

Instead of trying to dig and scratch with his feet and only sink deeper, he thought that if he could roll back and forth, or even all the way over, he could get out of this place.

He leaned to the right and noticed that his side which had hurt so badly a few days ago was now only faintly sore. He leaned to the left with even more success. A shiver of delight passed over his body. He began to talk to himself. "Now to the right. Now to the left. Now a half twist." In no time at all he was planning his next act for the fall of the great hickory. "There she was, folks. Straight and tall. But all of a sudden she leaned to the right. Then to the left. Back to the right. Left. Right. Then she gave a twist as if trying to go in both directions at once. And, all at once—all at once—" Skunky gave a mighty effort and then shouted triumphantly, "All at once there she was, folks, on the ground!"

And there Skunky was, free of his concealment, stretched out on top of the ground, prone as a dead tree but inwardly as excited as a bee in season's first clover.

Again he called, loud as he could, "Anyone around here?"

All was still quiet, save for the sky butterfly which sounded much louder and much lower than Skunky had ever heard. He looked up through the tree branches, but they were too thick for him to see anything flying in the sky.

"There is no one around here," he said to himself, as if stating Item No. 1 of his predicament. "Therefore," he continued, raising his voice so he could hear himself above the now really quite boisterous chugging of the sky creature, "I must try to find some food. Secondly, I must groom my fur. What a mess I am! Thirdly, I must get back to the hickory stump. Fourthly—"

Skunky never got to his "fourthly," for off in the woods to his left was the loudest noise he had ever heard. It sounded as if a hundred dead hickories were falling, each one knocking over several trees around it. It kept getting closer and closer. "A windstorm," Skunky whispered, shivering now with fear. But the sun was still making lacy patches on the woodland floor.

It was quite puzzling. Skunky was torn between

131

curiosity and fear. The noise was like a thousand Crack-Splat-Slam-Whomps! The crashing, smashing, banging was so loud and near, he was forced to cover his ears with his paws. He crept back to the log which had concealed him for so long and tried to get back under it.

All at once the noise was over, and, if possible, the forest was quieter than ever.

"Fourthly," Skunky continued, trying to act as if nothing frightening had happened, "fourthly—where was I? Oh, yes, back at the hickory stump. Fourthly, I must thank my friends." He started in the direction of the hickory stump, but had gone only a little way when, fairly exploding with curiosity, he turned and started in the direction of the big noise, mentally moving all his plans up a notch and starting again. "Firstly, I must see what that was!"

He crept cautiously toward where the big noise had been, stopping every now and then to look around. Soon he noticed broken branches and twigs on the ground, their leaves still green and shining. These got thicker and thicker until he came out into a little place where the whole tops of the trees were broken off. Then, through an opening in some brush, he saw a strange thing. There, in the middle of a little clearing, a sky butterfly had landed. Or, more likely, fallen. It looked rather broken up, but then he really hadn't ever seen one close, so couldn't tell for sure.

Closer and closer he crept, ready to turn and run at the slightest threatening motion and noise. The sun glistened on the creature's enormous wings, which surely must be broken, Skunky decided. He climbed up on one and waited to see if anything would happen. When it didn't, he climbed on toward the body. Seeing a hole in the side, he poked his nose in and looked around. It was all very strange. Knobs and levers and metal and wires all mixed up together.

There was an ominous sputtering sound, the kind Skunky had heard when a fire was burning in the Deep Forest. He looked around and saw fire sparks coming from tangled wires. It frightened him, and Skunky did what he always did when frightened. He sent a spray of his protective perfume. The sparks stopped.

But no sooner was the fright over when another one came. Something stirred. Skunky observed closely. Perhaps it was the heart of this sky butterfly, but it looked strangely like a Man. Hard to tell, though, the way it was all crumpled.

When the thing made a grunting sound, Skunky released some more perfume. Then he heard a noise from outside. He hurried back to the hole and looked out. Some Men were running right toward him, talking excitedly. There was no way for Skunky to escape without jumping out in front of them. He turned back and made his way as quickly and quietly as he could to the tail end of the sky butterfly.

Seeing what looked like another hole in the side, Skunky tried to jump through it but found, painfully, that it was covered with some glasslike substance. Just as he was about to move on for a better hiding place, a small motion outside caught his eye. He looked at it closely and soon made out the head of Mr. Raccoon peering from behind one of the broken trees. Skunky waved. Mr. Raccoon nodded his head only slightly, and Skunky recognized Mr. Raccoon's need to be cautious with any telltale motions.

Soon Skunky made out the form of Mrs. Raccoon behind another tree. And there was Squirrel up on a branch. And Chipmunk over there. And Chuck! He was so glad to see his old friends, he waved vigorously. Mrs. Raccoon's eyes seemed as big as hedge apples. Chuck sat with both hands in the air in an attitude of outlandish surprise, and Squirrel, for the first time, was speechless.

They can't believe it is me, Skunky thought, and to reassure his friends, he stood up and turned around slowly to show that it really was him. He waved and formed silent words with his lips and was about to put on a pantomine of his tree falling act when he saw that his friends were silently disappearing. The Men who had entered the sky butterfly were dragging the crumpled, grunting manlike thing from it. They were saying things like "Whew" and "Phew" and "Mercy" and "My" and "Hoo-boy!"

Then came more Men. They put the crumpled, grunting manlike creature on a flat-looking bed and carried him away. Others stayed to walk around the broken butterfly, poking and punching. When Skunky saw some of them crawling in the hole, he scampered

134

over sharp-edged metal and through other gouging, splintery things to find as dark a hiding place as he could.

Hours passed. Skunkys' legs cramped, and his stomach ached with hunger. Sometimes it seemed his head was detached from his body and going around and around in a whirlwind. He longed to be back under the log in the dirt and dead leaves. This hard jabbing unfamiliar material that bruised his sides wasn't friendly like the earth and leaves.

It was long after dark before the voices of the Men ceased. When all had been quiet for some time, Skunky emerged from his hiding place and crept to the hole that led to the outside. Bright moonlight softened the broken trees, tipped all the leaves with silver, and made pretty shadows on the ground. There was a low drone of nighttime insects and a soft gentleness in the air.

Remembering his friends out there somewhere, Skunky felt very good and started to climb out the hole by which he had entered. At that moment a Man came around the end of the broken butterfly. Skunky had to dart back in.

Back and forth went the Man, and around and around. Occasionally something in his hand would send a beam of light across broken branches and tangled wreckage. At first Skunky thought it was one of those sticks Men carried that barked fire, but there was no bark, only a beam of light snapping on and off. Once the beam of light was turned toward the surrounding trees and there, caught in the beam, was, unmistakably, Mr. Raccoon's eyes. Skunky would have recognized them anywhere. The Man started toward them. Skunky wanted to yell, "Run, Mr. Raccoon!" But the eyes held unblinkingly.

Suddenly it came to Skunky that Mr. Raccoon was

deliberately luring the Man away to give him time to escape. Quickly he crawled out the hole and darted to the first bit of wreckage he saw. It was all very noisy, and the beam of light came back to rest on his new hiding place.

A squall off to the right caused the beam of light to shift again. That's Mrs. Raccoon, Skunky thought, smiling as he made another dart across a little open space to a broken branch lying on the ground. The light came back in time to catch the tip end of his tail in its beam.

If he could put out fire sparks with his perfume, perhaps he could put out a light, Skunky thought, and was about ready to try as the light came closer and closer.

A chirring overhead made the light go up and there, plain as day, was Squirrel darting about in the shattered treetops. Good old Squirrel who hardly ever ventured out after dark.

Skunky ran to another hiding place while Squirrel kept the attention of the light. This time he was very near to where the trees and brush stood thick and unbroken. Now that his escape seemed sure, Skunky began to enjoy this little game. However, with his final dash to safety he did not linger, but made his way straight as he could to the hickory stump at the edge of the Grassy Meadow. Arriving well before any of the others, he ate some scraps of food he found around the old stump and then climbed on top and fell fast asleep.

17

Rabbit and Little Mocker Leave the Next County

Miles away in the Next County, Rabbit and Little Mocker were sleeping too, although the eastern sky was already pink and gold with morning. They had retired early the evening before to get as much sleep and rest as they could, for tomorrow was to be a big day. They were going to leave this place!

Their plan for leaving had taken shape after the same snarling, meowing creature that had sent Rabbit underground came back a second time, more fearsome than ever. Again Rabbit had had to dive under the rocks, and Little Mocker struggled for a place of safety.

All afternoon the threatening menace lay in the grass near Rabbit's hiding place, waiting for him to come out, not knowing that the noisy bird perched overhead would give the signal when it was safe for Rabbit to emerge. Near sundown, perhaps thinking he could do better down by the river, the creature quietly got up and walked away.

"Little Mocker," said Rabbit when the two had got together again, "we've got to leave this place."

Little Mocker was silent. That had been uppermost in his mind ever since he had stumbled into this dreary territory, but he knew that for him it was impossible. Countless times during the many weeks he had been here, he had tried. Day after day, pretending there was nothing wrong, he had lifted his wings and taken off from various perches only to fall to the ground in a terrible awkward mass of ruffled feathers. The falls knocked the breath from him and bruised his body so that he was always sore and stiff and limping. He could not even walk away. His gait was too slow. Should he be caught out in open spaces, with no nearby low branches to scrabble up, something would put a quick end to him.

"Rabbit, you must go alone," Little Mocker said. "I will come later." He tried to sound cheerful and even punctuated his statement with the newest little song he had made up, which was quite cheerful and one he planned to use when friends were sorrowful or downhearted—that is, if he ever had any more friends, now that Rabbit was leaving.

"We will go together," Rabbit said with such authority that Little Mocker half-hoped there was a way, although try as he might, he couldn't think of any. After a while he asked in a small unsteady voice, "How?"

Rabbit didn't answer immediately. He hopped around, as if trying out his sore legs, ate a few sparse sprigs of clover, hopped around some more, stretched his legs one at a time, then announced, "You will ride on my back."

Little Mocker didn't know whether to laugh or cry. The idea of his riding on Rabbit's back, managing to stay on during those high quick leaps, seemed utterly ridiculous. He could just see himself being bounced off, taking long arching nosedives, landing even harder than he had during his own attempts at flight. But the fact that Rabbit wanted to be burdened with him when he could go on alone was so touching that it made a lump in his throat.

"Rabbit, I don't think I can."

"We'll see," said Rabbit. "First thing in the morning, we'll see." His eyes had been full of wisdom, and his ears moved expressively.

And now it was morning. Little Mocker, who had had difficulty in going to sleep, heard Rabbit saying, "Wake up. Wake up! This is the day we are leaving. This is the day we are starting for home!" There was such excitement in his voice, it was hard for Little Mocker not to be excited and hopeful too.

"Breakfast first," said Rabbit, hopping around much more alertly after another night's rest. "Then away we go!" He took an exceedingly high, far leap to prove that he was quite ready. Little Mocker couldn't tell for sure, but he thought he saw a small, quickly erased grimace of pain.

When they had found a few suitable things to eat, although a far cry from breakfasts they had each known back home at the Grassy Meadow, Rabbit shook the dew from his feet, tweaked his whiskers, flipped his ears, and said, "All right, mount up, Little Mocker!"

"Oh, Rabbit, dear friend, I know I can't stay on your back. But I thank you for this kind thought."

"From now on, we will not use the word 'can't,' " said Rabbit, looking very serious. "Now get on."

Obediently, Little Mocker climbed onto Rabbit's back.

"Now, which way would you say we should go?" asked Rabbit.

Little Mocker lifted a wing to point in the direction from which Rabbit had come. As he did, another wing feather fell out. He looked at it lying there on the ground, glistening in the morning sun. Had he had time to give it much thought, he might have become quite sad, feeling that he was losing what good feathers he had left, but Rabbit was saying, "Get set! Go!"

Rabbit made a long leap, as if to set a speed that

139

might get them home before dark. Little Mocker went arching high into the air and landed headfirst in a tangle of prickly thistles, three feet in front of Rabbit.

"Get back on," Rabbit commanded before Little Mocker had even had time to spit all the dirt, leaves, and prickles out of his mouth.

"Rabbit, I really don't think—" Little Mocker began, but was interrupted by Rabbit who again commanded, "Get back on."

Little Mocker climbed back on. When he was well situated, Rabbit took another leap. Although it was much shorter than the first, once again Little Mocker went somersaulting through the air over Rabbit's head, this time landing on his back. He shook himself to straighten his feathers and twisted his neck, wondering if it might not be half broken. Looking around for Rabbit, he saw that he was crouching right in front of him, indicating wordlessly that he expected Little Mocker to try again.

Wearily Little Mocker tried again and again and again. When he saw that Rabbit was determined not to give up, he began to try different things. When the two of them were at the highest point of the leaping arch, Little Mocker tried to lift himself from Rabbit's back and then settle back down softly before Rabbit's feet touched the ground, but he couldn't land in a balanced way and slid off to the right or left time after time. Then he tried bracing himself forward on Rabbit's upleap and quickly bracing backward on the downward arch in a sort of rocking motion.

The sun was high in the sky before he got the tiniest little idea that he might be making some improvement.

"Dig your claws into my fur when you feel you're falling off," Rabbit suggested.

When they tried this, in combination with the other movements Little Mocker was perfecting, he managed to stay on for several trial leaps. But he noted that when he had to curl his toenails into Rabbit's fur, little bits of fur came out and floated away.

"Rabbit, I must not do this," Little Mocker protested. "All your fur might be gone before we get back to the Grassy Meadow."

"My fur will grow back," Rabbit assured. "Get back on."

This time Little Mocker stayed on for six rather long leaps.

"That's good," Rabbit complimented. "Even if you have to remount every six leaps, we can cover a good deal of territory in a day's time and maybe get out of here. But we must stay away from open territory so that if you should be dismounted at an inopportune time we could—" His voice trailed off.

"Save our necks from some killer," Little Mocker finished, realistically.

They crawled through the rusty wire fence that had saved Rabbit from Dog that first day he had arrived in the Next County and made their way to the outer edge of the thicket, where Rabbit stopped and said, "Here is where we start."

Little Mocker did not even turn to have a last look at the place where he had spent so many fearful, hungry, friendless days. The only good thing that had happened here, until Rabbit came, was the passing through of other birds from whom he had stolen snatches of song. Which reminded him—maybe a little song right now would be in order, a sort of encouraging, press-ahead, marching song. He flitted to Rabbit's back and began to sing.

Leapety, leapety, leapety, they went. Little Mocker rocked, rolled, jolted, slid, and bounced, but didn't miss a note of his song and managed in some miraculous way to stay on, although there were times, when Rabbit was at the height of his leap, that Little Mocker found himself swaying far to each side and once all the way underneath Rabbit.

Thus they went for half a mile before Rabbit stopped for a rest. "Crackety! That singing is a splendid idea," he complimented Little Mocker. "Have you noticed how it keeps us in time with each other?"

Little Mocker was so choked with happiness that this thing was going to work, that he might actually be going back home, he could not reply. He just kept on singing while tears ran down his beak and fell to the ground.

Rabbit pretended not to see and stretched out for a little rest before pressing forward. He fixed an eye on a distant wooded ridge and thought that by nightfall they might be there, although whether it was the way he had come, he did not know.

18
The Brass Trimmed Box Is Brought to the Grassy Meadow

Back at the Grassy Meadow, Skunky twitched in his sleep, felt a cozy warmth touching his body, stirred comfortably, and finally opened his eyes to see that it was broad daylight, that Mrs. Raccoon's Flower Garden quilt had been tucked around him, and that all his friends were standing in a silent circle around the stump.

When they saw that Skunky was finally awake, the friends clapped their paws, danced a polka, and shouted gladly, "Skunky's back. Skunky's back. Skunky who was gone is back."

The frogs, who had found the morning sun too hot for their tender backs, swirled their lily-pad umbrellas in shiny green circles and the meadow mice, standing on each other's shoulders, made high acrobatic pyramids.

When the noise and chatter quieted, Mrs. Raccoon spoke. "Why did they take you away, and where to, Skunky?"

"Take me away? Where to?" Skunky repeated, having no notion what Mrs. Raccoon meant.

"That big thing that fell in the woods," Mrs. Raccoon explained. "We saw you inside it. Did they take you away and then bring you back? Tell us everything, Skunky."

It came to Skunky as Mrs. Raccoon talked that it

must have appeared to his friends that he had been taken away somewhere. He knew they had searched for him and, not finding him, must have assumed that he had been skunknapped. Glory! What a good story he could make of this. Much better than the fall of the old hickory. And it could have ever so many more variations. He could describe the thousand and one countries he had been to, the innumerable narrow escapes he had had, as well as the many honours that had been bestowed upon him, the lectures he had delivered, the crimes he had solved, the oratorical contests he had won, the Oak Ball clusters he'd received for acting!

Skunky's eyes twinkled. He rubbed his hands with anticipated delight, drew himself up to his full height, and began. "Yes sir, folks, there I was, tumbled out of that old trap in a mighty aching heap when you all pulled it over the log, and let me say thanks, right now, for that mighty effort." Skunky looked ashamed that he'd been a little late with his thanks and proceeded to overdo it a bit, going around to shake hands with everyone there and repeating over and over his heartfelt thanks and telling them also what a fine game that was they played last night, diverting the attention of the Man with the light so he could get away. When he felt he had this all duly attended to, he proceeded.

"Yes, no less than a minute after I'd been dumped there by the log, here this mighty sky butterfly came swooping down—"

"That was an aeroplane," said Head Frog. "A-E-R-O-P-L-A-N-E. I've seen pictures of them in old newspapers down at the dump."

"Here this mighty aeroplane swooped down," Skunky continued, it making no difference to him what the thing was called.

"We heard it," said one of the little 'possums who was now old enough to talk.

"Just so many feet from the ground," Skunky continued, motioning to an area that would have been above local tree level, "it let down a lasso and got me around my neck." Here he paused to reflect, and thinking this a bit risky to be lassoed around the neck, amended his statement, a thing he did rather well, as all things are after much practice. "Around my waist rather, and quick as a flash I was up and inside that thing, and away we went!"

Skunky looked up for a suitable point in the sky and, seeing a fleecy little cloud, informed his audience that behind that cloud was a country the likes of which he had never seen before. He rolled his eyes significantly. "Streets are of green jade with delicate edgings of crocheted gold, set with glistening stones as blue as Mrs. Raccoon's Vicks jar and red as sour gum leaves in the autumn. Everything was so sparkling clean it hurt my eyes. There were fountains of lemonade with crystal cups to drink from just about everywhere you looked. Corn dogs. Hush puppies. Scrabbledobies."

"What?" went up a chorus of demanding questions.

"Scrabbledobies," Skunky repeated, feeling very smug that he was still able to make up such a fine word and hold an audience after his recent bad experience. "Very good, they are. You take crushed hickory nuts and a dab of honey." Skunky scratched his head as if trying his best to remember the recipe for scrabbledobies.

Into the small silence, Chipmunk asked, "Was Rabbit with you?"

"Rabbit? Why no, Rabbit wasn't with me." Skunky looked around and noted that Rabbit wasn't there.

"Where is Rabbit?" he asked, sorry that old Rabbit had missed the first part of his story.

A sad silence fell upon the crowd. The temporary enchantment of the story was over. "We last saw Rabbit when he pulled out of the trap-tugging line and went bounding off in the direction of oncoming Dog," said Mr. Raccoon.

Skunky came down out of his cloud country quickly to share the concern of the others. "No tracks? No tufts of fur anywhere?" he asked.

"No tracks. No tufts," Mother 'Possum said, shaking her head sadly.

"But we's got a machine that's gonna tell us where Rabbit is," spoke up Aleen Meadow Mouse in a happier tone of voice. "It would have told us where you were too, Skunky, only it's got to be mended. It will tell the answer to anything."

All eyes turned to Aleen Meadow Mouse. Some thought she was trying to outdo Skunky, but all the other meadow mice and frogs who had helped pull the Little Toy Computer out of the dump pile took up parts of the song they had made up: "Light the lights. Push the buttons. Ask a question. Get the answer. Exactly."

Finally D.P. hopped upon the stump and motioned for attention. "It is true," he said. "It was found in my most intricate mansion with its maze of interesting tunnels, hallways, balconies, game rooms, salons, studies, and inglenooks by the fire." He looked around to enjoy any possible admiring gestures or countenances, for he knew there were some who did not admire the structure, smell, or design of his large rambling home where one wing or another was almost always on fire. Then, to keep things strictly honest, which he made a habit of doing, for he knew some rats had built up a reputation for telling lies, he said, "It was really Mrs. Raccoon who

146

first found it, some time ago." He looked at Mrs. Raccoon and gave an appreciative bow. "You might say I re-found it. It is called a Little Toy Computer and needs some batteries before we can get it to work. Tell them what it says on the side, Head Frog."

Head Frog, who had memorized every word, stepped forward and repeated, " 'When all buttons are pushed and all lights burning, ask any question of me and I will have the answer.' On the underneath side it says, 'Open this door to replace regular flashlight batteries.' "

"Incredible!" said Mrs. Raccoon, holding up both hands in an expression of awe.

"Unbelievable!" whispered Mother 'Possum, too overcome with what she had heard to speak aloud.

There were other barely audible expressions such as "Glory be!" "Hallelujah!" "Pop my pawpaws!" "Hot berries!" and "Creepin' crawdaddies!"

Chipmunk, more excited than he had ever been, said, "I just never, ever been in my life heard about such a truth that tells machine to any question."

Then came a silence as the full import of this

147

marvelous machine crept into the furthermost recesses of their minds. Even the little crickets around ceased to sing, and locusts wound down to a complete stop. The inhabitants of the Grassy Meadow, Deep Forest, and Rustling Brook sat bewildered, entranced, fascinated.

Into this stillness, Chuck spoke, voicing the question now on the minds of everyone present. "What's a flashlight battery?"

Everyone looked at each other questioningly and waited for someone to speak. When it was apparent that no one knew what a flashlight battery was, faces that had so recently been happy began to grow glum again. Each had had so many personal questions he would like to have asked the computer, so he could settle things in his own head and get on with living, to say nothing of the most pressing questions right now: Where was Rabbit? Was he still alive?

"Now what we will have to do," said Mr. Raccoon in the familiar voice that had so often calmed them all, "is open that little door and see what a flashlight battery looks like. I would assume there might still be some inside it, only broken or worn out."

"True," agreed D.P. "But so far we cannot get the door open. There have been other pressing things to divide our attention."

"Quite so," said Mr. Raccoon. "But if this thing can give us the answer to everything, then it would seem that all our efforts should be bent toward getting it to work."

"Try as we might, we couldn't open the door," said Head Frog. "It will take someone with a strong grip and cunning fingers."

Everyone looked at Mrs. Raccoon, who had so successfully placed the splints and wrapped the bindings for so many broken legs and wings. She also had screwed shiny lids off bottles, sprung steel traps, and

148

even pulled a fishhook from one of the frogs' hind legs without causing any damage at all. Now she flexed her fingers, testing their strength and nimbleness, and said, "I'll try."

Away they went, so fast that a little whirlwind of dust and leaves was created, causing the meadow mice to sneeze and the frogs to hop to the outer limits of the procession so as to see better.

When they arrived at the place where the Little Toy Computer sat, its brass corners reflecting the sun's rays and the painted designs appearing brighter than ever, everyone became very still, and even tiptoed around it, and felt obliged to sit in quiet reverence for a while in the presence of this thing that had the incomprehensible power to answer all questions.

After a while Mrs. Raccoon arose, rubbed her hands on her seven-ringed tail, a thing she did when important matters like this were presented to her, and approached the Little Toy Computer. There was such a silence, one could hear the breathing of the very youngest meadow mouse.

Caps and knobs usually opened things by turning them to the right, Mrs. Raccoon had learned, so she tried that first. The little knob did not move a fraction of an inch. She tried turning it to the left with no better results. Grasping it with both hands and summoning all the muscle power she could, she tried it again. There was no movement at all. With her dainty fingers, she picked away little flakes of rust to see if there was a keyhole. Some things, she knew, had locks. Finding no keyhole, she looked for things to push or slide up, down, or crosswise. After a long trial of everything she could imagine, she turned to her audience and said, "It appears to me that the knob that opens the door is rusted. It will need some oil."

Relieved that there was a possible solution, every-

149

one began to offer suggestions as to where one might find oil. Some said there was oil along the road that led to the dump pile. Others remembered that up at the barn where Dog lived was a can of grease. Skunky had even heard that they all had oil in their bodies in the form of fat, but how to get it out was most perplexing.

No one noticed D.P.'s disappearance and all were still noisily discussing where oil might be found when he was back, holding aloft a half-empty jar of something that Head Frog pronounced to be Vaseline. "V-A-S-E-L-I-N-E."

When they were all seated again in respectful silence, Mrs. Raccoon applied the Vaseline to the rusty places on the little door, waited a while, tried again, and all at once somersaulted backward three times, so hard had she pulled and so easily had the door suddenly opened.

A great cheer went up from the assembled crowd.

Head Frog, D.P., and Mr. Raccoon stepped forward. Inside the opened door they saw four little round objects, each about the length of a small pawpaw. There was printing on them, so Head Frog hopped forward, shading his eyes so as to see better.

"That's it," he exclaimed, puffing up with such joy and pride he could hardly continue. "These are flashlight batteries. It says so on the side. F-L-A-S-H—" he began to spell.

"Oh, never mind the spelling," Chuck interrupted. "What else does it say, if anything?"

Head Frog read on, " 'Guaranteed. 30p each. No. 950. Size D8.' "

"It would appear," said Mr. Raccoon after a moment or two of thought, "that one or more of these batteries are worn out and that when they are replaced, this computer will work."

Again a cheer went up, but not quite so long this

time, and it trailed off more quickly as misgivings about where the batteries could be obtained began to penetrate the more thoughtful minds. Finally Mrs. Raccoon voiced the question. "Where do we get them, and how can we tell which ones are no good?"

To the latter, there seemed to be no answer since all the batteries looked the same—no splits, slits, nicks, cracks, or crevices. But D.P. ventured to say that surely somewhere in his many-storeyed castle there would be flashlight batteries. He heaved a sigh which was echoed by all the rest as they looked at the dump and contemplated the idea of finding flashlight batteries.

"Just think," said Squirrel, who hadn't had much to say all day, "if this computer was working, we could ask it where to find the batteries," which to some seemed to be a fairly dumb thing to say, although they had good manners enough not to say so.

Mr. Raccoon climbed to the top of the computer, the better to be seen by all, turned his face toward the dump pile, raised an arm pointing in that direction, and shouted, "Onward!" The single word was so full of determination, so promising of victory, that everyone, regardless of their fears of darkness, cave-ins, suffocation, tight places, or being lost in mazes, started toward D.P.'s castle.

19
Little Mocker Flies Again

The first day's search for the batteries passed with no results, as did the second and the third. Days stretched into weeks, weeks into months. Mrs. Raccoon suggested that the Little Toy Computer should not be left sitting out in the weather. Even if it took five, ten, fifteen years or longer to find batteries, she felt it was of upmost importance to save it. Some future generation, even beyond their children or their children's children, might come into possession of the batteries and live in that wonderful state of having access to answers for all their questions.

So D.P., who knew exactly where there was a discarded little wagon, brought it alongside the computer and with the help of many others tugged, pushed, slid, ooched, and squooched it into the wagon. They took it to the edge of the Grassy Meadow near the white oak home of the Raccoons. There they mounted it on wooden blocks so one could not only get all around it, but underneath it too. They also built a shelter of brush over it which not only protected it from rain, wind, and hail, but hid it from the eyes of any passing strangers who might, in their curiosity, jiggle, jabble, and jumble the thing to pieces. Clever little camou-flaged doorways were left in the shelter so the local neighbours could go in at any time to not only contemplate the potential power of the computer, but also to enjoy the design and shine of the brass corners, the brightly painted designs, and what lights they could get to flash by pressing the assortment of buttons.

Whenever Mrs. Raccoon was cleaning her own house, she always cleaned the computer too, as if it were a part of her own furniture. She oiled the hinges and the knob to the little door so it wouldn't rust shut again. She polished the brass with wood ashes and cleaned the sides with water and soapwort roots. Quite often after she had it gleaming she would sit down beside it to rest and wonder, if it were working, what she would ask it. Some days it seemed that the only good and obvious question was, "What shall I make for supper?" Other days, when in a more reflective mood, she felt there should be a larger, more important question, an all-purpose question, the answer to which would unlock so many of the world's mysteries.

One day, thinking herself to be alone inside the brush shelter, she voiced a question aloud, not meaning it for the computer, but just voicing a question that so often nagged at the edges of her mind. "I wonder whatever became of Little Mocker."

"Who's Little Mocker?" asked a squeaky voice.

Mrs. Raccoon jumped with surprise, thinking the computer had suddenly spoken, but hearing a rustling in the thatched roof overhead, she looked up to see the head of a tiny meadow mouse thrust down through the dried straw and weeds.

"Which one are you?" she asked, since most of the meadow mice looked alike.

"I'm Lauren."

"Then you've been born since Little Mocker left. He was a bird we found with a broken wing who flew away."

"How could he fly away with a broken wing?" asked Lauren.

Mrs. Raccoon then told all about how she had mended the wing and of the day Little Mocker had flown away to get back to his family where he could learn to sing. "I sort of thought he'd come back some day," she sighed.

"Maybe he will," squeaked little Lauren, trying to comfort Mrs. Raccoon, whom she thought looked sad today.

At that moment, far, far away, going in the wrong direction, although they didn't know it, Little Mocker and Rabbit were leapety-leapetying along, trying to get back to the Grassy Meadow. After weeks and weeks of travel, they did much better coordinating their motions. Still, there were times when Rabbit had to swerve quickly in midair to keep from coming down on an unforeseen rock or prickly bush. Little Mocker, riding lightly, his mind on things like whether it was right to steal songs, say one thing and mean another, and a whole host of other bothersome questions, would land in a clumsy heap with his breath knocked out of him. After such spills, he would ride for a while with his toenails curled tighter in Rabbit's fur, although he did hate to see those little wisps of Rabbit's fur blowing away in the breeze. More and more he insisted on walking for long stretches at a time.

One day they were walking along, side by side, chatting pleasantly, when, rounding a corner of a thicket more quickly than usual, standing directly in their path and towering above them was a bear.

Little Mocker gulped and said, "I'm sorry, sir," in a very high-pitched, quavery voice. "We rounded that corner a little faster than is our custom."

Seeing that the stranger was making no move to

swat them, Little Mocker kept on talking and talking as if that was what was keeping the big fellow from knocking them lollapolloosa. He told the stranger how they were trying to get back to an old home they'd been away from for so long, of how pleasant life was there, everyone looking out for the good of all. When he had run out of breath and was taking another big gulp to go at it again, the bear spoke. "It is I who am in the way. I rather hog the trails and really should be made to wear a sign saying, WIDE LOAD." He chuckled, and his rich dark fur rippled in the sunlight.

Little Mocker and Rabbit thought it was the most beautiful sound they'd ever heard. Not for weeks, save for their own feeble attempts, had they heard any good-natured laughter or exchanged a civil word with passing strangers.

That same day, not long afterwards, they passed two meadow mice, walking along primly, carrying sprigs of wild asters. They bowed politely as good meadow mice do and made pleasant remarks about the quality of the day before moving on.

At evening they came to a stream of water, rippling along between ferny banks. Not a single bottle, can, or plastic cup floated on top. The water was so clear that, bending over to take a drink, Rabbit saw a frog sitting way down amongst the polished stones. He couldn't be sure, but it did seem as though the frog winked at him.

When they had drunk their fill and were settling in for the night underneath the shelter of a hazelnut bush, Little Mocker said, his voice choked with emotion, "Rabbit, I think that we are out of that Next County."

As if he had walked through a Valley of Darkness and Death and had come out safe and sound on the other side, Rabbit, not trusting his own voice, merely nodded in affirmation and whisked away tears of gratitude and thankfulness.

The next day the two friends had another, even more exciting experience. Wishing to make as much progress as they could, Little Mocker was riding on Rabbit's back, and Rabbit, excited by being in friendly territory again, was making very high, wide, and handsome leaps. Little Mocker, having to hold on tight, noticed more and more wisps of Rabbit's fur floating away behind them. He hoped Rabbit was right when he had said that his fur would eventually grow back.

Mulling over this fact, it came to Little Mocker that if Rabbit's fur grew back, why didn't his own feathers grow back, although, of course, fur and feathers were quite different. Out of curiosity he raised his wing to look where that first broken flight feather had fallen out. What he saw caused him to gasp and tumble off backward in a feathery ball of surprise and wonderment. A nice long feather was growing back in the same place where the other one had fallen out. And there was another one coming in behind it where the second broken feather had fallen out. Hastily he raised his other wing only to find more new wing feathers.

"What is it?" Rabbit asked, having stopped and turned around when he felt Little Mocker fall off.

"Rabbit!" Little Mocker exclaimed. "My flying feathers are growing back. Look!" He raised his wings to show where the broken feathers had been replaced and that there were new ones on the opposite wing where seemingly perfectly good ones had fallen out.

Rabbit was as happy as Little Mocker, for he knew how sad his friend had been. "Can you fly now?" he asked.

"Oh, Rabbit, do you suppose I can? Do you suppose I've been riding along these many days without even trying? I have noticed that I've been able to keep my balance better."

"Well, try!" urged Rabbit, seeing no reason to delay.

Little Mocker walked around, undecided. He wanted to try, and yet he didn't. Suppose he couldn't? Suppose even though new flight feathers had grown back, they might somehow have the same conditions as the old broken ones, and he'd just go around and around in those tiresome, everlasting circles?

"Even if you can't fly, you can still sing those wonderful songs," Rabbit said, preparing Little Mocker for any forthcoming disappointment, should there be any. "And I'll always be around if you have to get anywhere in a hurry."

Little Mocker continued to pace back and forth. He looked at the grass bending in the breeze, the nearby treetops gently swaying, a cloud floating by. And for the first time since he'd left the Grassy Meadow, he heard the musical notes of the little breezes drawing long floating spiderwebs across the wayside asters, heard them whisper, "Come on, Little Mocker. You can fly. Just lift your wings. Apple orchards are awaiting you. Fields of ripening grain. Dewy hill, blue with morning mist." And once again Little Mocker, in a blissful response, said, "I will. I will."

He fluttered his wings, felt the good rush of air they created, fluttered them some more, lifted slowly at first, then faster and faster, higher and higher. A rapture of delight tingled up and down his spine, then spread out into his wings. He felt light as thistledown. Up and down and round and round he went, dipping, swaying, swinging, making scallops and circles, slants and dives, all in perfect control.

Rabbit, seeing all the aerial acrobatics and being

so happy for Little Mocker, cut some fancy didoes himself. He ran around in complicated curlycues, leaped extraordinary distances, turned double somersaults, bucked and jackknifed and performed every feat he could think of.

When Little Mocker landed, the two friends looked long at each other, then fell over and rolled in the grass, laughing and crying and laughing again until they were quite exhausted.

20
Little Mocker Meets His Brother Songer

Some time that night, after the moon was quite high, Little Mocker awoke. Wondering if it had all been a dream, he tried his wings and was flooded all over again with the sweet discovery that he could indeed fly. He flew to the top of a nearby tree and poured out such a rich melody of song that every nearby sleeping creature awoke and came out of his little burrow or bed to listen. Every busy member of the nighttime population, making his own chatter, chirrup, or rustling, grew quiet. To the troubled, it was like a gentle hand laid on their hearts to cool the fever of care. To the sorrowful, it brought a curious joy.

Little Mocker's song spoke of lonely, heart-sore hours (he had known so many), of doubt and fear, disappointments, hunger, and worry. But each phrase ended on a gloriously beautiful, triumphant note, telling of the overcoming of these sad things, of love and friendship, hope, unconquerable courage, and the goodness of being alive. So merry and joyous were the notes that some of those listening peered from behind their sheltering bushes to see if there weren't actually golden bubbles floating in the moonlight.

When his concert was over, Little Mocker put his head beneath his wing, spoke to the Keeper, and was almost asleep when he felt the branch upon which he was perched quiver. He opened his eyes, saw nothing, decided it was the nighttime breeze stirring amongst the leaves. But there it was again! Soon he made out the form of another bird out near the end of the branch. He watched for a while and saw that the bird was inching closer and closer. He noticed, in the still bright light of the moon, that it looked very much like himself—grey coat, darker wings and tail, both with white bars, and a whitish breast.

The fear that had gripped Little Mocker for so long began to tense his muscles and make the feathers around his neck stand out in alarm. Then, remembering he was out of that fearsome Next County, he spoke with friendly cheerfulness. "Hello."

"Oh, sir," said the stranger, "I hope I did not awaken you, but I did wish to tell you that your songs are the most beautiful I have ever heard."

"Thank you," said Little Mocker. "I see that we must be of the same kind, so I assume that you sing too."

"Some," replied the stranger. "But not nearly so well. Never ever will there be anyone who sings as well. Are you just passing through on the migration?"

"Just passing through," replied Little Mocker, "but not on the migration. A friend and I are trying to get back to a place we once knew, but have been wandering around for many weeks now looking for it."

"Where could that be? Perhaps I could help."

Little Mocker's heart leaped. "A place called the Grassy Meadow through which runs the Rustling Brook. It is bordered by the Deep Forest. Have you heard of it?"

"Those places are not familiar to me. Were you born there?"

"No. I was born in a lilac bush somewhere. But because I learned early to fly well, and perhaps showing off a bit, I flew too far away, became lost, met with an accident, and have never been able to find my old home, my parents, brother, or sister."

"I, too, was born in a lilac bush," exclaimed the stranger, "and go back there every year as we come north. In fact, it is not very far from here."

Little Mocker went on to tell how he had been injured in the fall of the big hickory and how other creatures had befriended him. He thought that the visiting bird was beginning to act in a strange way, twisting and flitting as if he were bored with the story or else there was something very urgent on his mind he wished to say.

When Little Mocker began describing the day he left the Grassy Meadow in search of his first home, the strange bird, as if not being able to stand it any longer, interrupted with a shrill question. "Are you Little Mocker?"

"Why, yes, I am," said Little Mocker wonderingly.

"Then you must be my brother!"

163

For Little Mocker, who had already had so much excitement for one day, this was almost more than he could bear. When the strange bird sitting next to him identified himself as Songer, and gave the name of his sister, there was no doubt in Little Mocker's mind but that here indeed was his brother. His heart swelled within him until he thought it would burst. They wrapped their wings about each other. They cried. They laughed. They twittered and trilled and tumbled around in a feathery flurry of glowing warmth and delight.

Then the questions tumbled out of Little Mocker. "Mother? Father? Melody? So you are Songer? Where are the others?"

One by one, Songer answered, telling Little Mocker that the family was safe, but had grieved these many months, thinking he was forever lost. "They have already gone south for the winter, and I will be joining them soon. In fact, I plan to leave at first light. Come with me, Little Mocker."

Little Mocker thought for a long time. It would be so good to see his family, and now that he could fly again, it would be a pure pleasure to spend his days thus, winging his way merrily over the miles and miles of field and forest to the southland. Many of the birds passing through the Next County had spoken of its delights. But when he thought of Mr. and Mrs. Raccoon, Chuck, Skunky, Squirrel, D.P., and all his other friends, not to mention a very special one not far below him, sleeping now, he shook his head and said, "No, I must get back to the Grassy Meadow."

Songer, who saw the mixed emotions on his brother's face, hastened to say, "Well, never mind, we'll all be back here come spring. You can meet us here."

Little Mocker brightened momentarily, then acknowledged in a small embarrassed voice, "I don't know where 'here' is, Songer. In fact, we're really lost and just wandering around, hoping to stumble onto some landmark we will recognize. I remember when I left the lilac bush, I flew for miles and miles, past a waterfall, past a railroad track—"

"Then you are very close, brother," Songer interrupted. "Come, I will show you where these are."

Together they flew from the tree, across a wide field of corn, rustling now in its late summer ripeness, through a small forest, around the edge of a ridge, and there, bright in the moonlight, was the cascading waterfall and a few miles beyond that a railroad track.

"Oh, Songer," exclaimed Little Mocker, his heart full of joy, "I think I know my way now." Far, far away to the north he saw the outline of a deep forest and knew that it must be home.

Songer then took Little Mocker several miles in the opposite direction to show him the lilac bush where they had both begun life. They sat on the nearby fence and sang duets for over an hour. After the strains of an especially sweet one had died away, Little Mocker asked, "Songer, do you know about the Keeper of All Creatures?"

"Oh, yes," Songer replied quickly. "It is for Him I sing."

"You do?"

"Mother said if we have any gift, we ought to use it for Him. And it does appear as if we mockers are singers, doesn't it?" He gave Mocker an approving look and added, "Some better than others. Tell me, brother, how did you learn to sing so well?"

Little Mocker did not answer for a long time. In fact, he thought of flying away without saying another word rather than reveal to his brother how he had come by his songs. He started to make up some story, tell a lie, but when he began to talk it was the truth he

165

blurted out. "I stole them. Snatched them right out of the air from other birds."

"But that isn't stealing," protested Songer, somewhat amused at Little Mocker's serious expression.

"It isn't?"

"No. That's our nature. That's the way Mother taught us. We just listened and learned. It's not stealing to watch or listen to someone else and then try to do better or put it all together in a new way."

Of all the good things that had happened to Little Mocker this day, he felt that this was the best. Since he had first mimicked that owl's "Who? Who?" he had had a guilty conscience. Being batted around, chewed on, hungry, scared, or knocked blind couldn't ever be as bad as a guilty conscience, he thought.

"Oh, Songer," he said, his voice quavering, "what a relief. You say it's our nature? It's the way we're made to do?"

"Exactly," assured Songer.

Little Mocker wondered if ever in his lifetime he would feel as good as he did this night. He jumped up and down on the limb, his skinny toes spread wide apart, and said, "It'll be my way to stomp out bad things."

"Stomp?" asked Songer, having come up against a new word.

When Little Mocker could stop reeling and tumbling in a feathered blur of bliss, all the while running the musical scale for two octaves, backwards and forwards, then doing it again, backtracking every third note to pick up a minor tone before proceeding, then working from both ends of the scale toward the middle, he breathlessly told Songer of his and Mrs. Raccoon's little impromptu stomping ritual and how they vowed to help stomp out evil. "Each in his own best way, Songer, and now I know that song is my best way, and I needn't worry about how I learned to do it."

When the sky was growing pink in the east, Songer said that he must go. "But I'll see you here again, come spring."

Little Mocker looked around to fix the place and the directions in his memory. "I'll be here, brother," he said.

Together they sang a last duet, then Songer lifted his wings, sailed around, dipped in a good-bye salute, and headed south.

Little Mocker watched him as far as he could see.

When the sun was touching the treetops with its golden fingers, Little Mocker descended to where Rabbit still lay sleeping. Nudging him gently awake, he said, "Rabbit, I know the way home now. I think it's not more than two days away."

Rabbit, who liked to wake up slowly, was instantly alert when he heard Little Mocker's words. "Home?" he said, and the word was like a sweet caress.

"Home," replied Little Mocker.

They ate a hasty breakfast and started out, this time not wandering aimlessly nor awkwardly with Little Mocker riding piggyback, but swiftly and with purpose. Little Mocker would fly overhead, guiding Rabbit, stop to wait for him to catch up, then fly some more, straight as an arrow toward the distant deep forest he had glimpsed in the night. He had so much to tell Rabbit about the night's happenings, but there would be time for that when they were resting. Right now it was "Forward!"

21
Mother 'Possum Finds a Flashlight

While Little Mocker and Rabbit had been wandering around trying to find their way home, back at the Grassy Meadow a search was still going on for flashlight batteries. Some searched in the daytime, others at night. In addition, all were still constantly on the alert for any sight, sound, or news of Rabbit. But despite their frustrations over the batteries and their great sorrow over Rabbit's absence, life had to go on. Food had to be gathered, children attended to, preparations made for a new season. It wouldn't be long before frost would put a white coating on the Grassy Meadow and the woods would get cold and windy, practising for winter and snow and ice and all that. So a degree of normality was returning.

Squirrel and Chipmunk began storing food for the coming winter. Over at the Shining River, Beaver started repairing his dam. The meadow mice were making intricate little tunnels to each other's houses through the drying grass, thinking it the greatest fun whenever they ran headfirst into each other as they made their circuitous little galleries.

Among other housecleaning chores, Mrs. Raccoon took her Flower Garden quilt to the Rustling Brook, washed it, and hung it to dry where others might come to admire and touch it, and go over again the old story of how she had salvaged it from the dump, a limp, dirty, thrown-away thing.

Mother 'Possum was still looking for a new home. One night when the moon was full and the air fragrant with ripening grapes, which gave her added zest, she thought she might venture as far as where the aeroplane had fallen. There might be some snapped-off trees in which she could find a nice, dry, hollow place.

Old Owl, hearing Mother 'Possum's footsteps, swooped down to a low branch to inquire, "Who? Whooo?" was going by. He had a very proprietary feeling about the night woods. But Mother 'Possum was so intent on her mission, she didn't even respond. Already she was visualizing a new home. It would be long and roomy with a front door and a back door and have a fresh smell.

She hadn't been to the site of the crash since the night they all gathered there to rescue Skunky and was surprised to see that all traces of the aeroplane had been removed. Only broken twigs and fallen branches still marked the spot.

Rounding the base of a stump, she stepped on something hard and felt a small sliding motion beneath her foot. Suddenly a bright beam of light started up amongst the grass. It scared her so, she rolled over on her side, became limp, shut her eyes, and looked very dead.

In a few minutes the nervous shock was over. She opened her eyes, only to see the beam of light still shining. She poked at the unusual object with her foot and sat for a long time beside it to see if it would coil and strike like a snake or hop off like a grasshopper. Deciding that it was harmless, she picked up a stick, brushed away the grass and leaves that were partially hiding it, and poked at it again, and then again. On one rather forceful jab the light went out. Another such jab in the opposite direction made it come back on.

Never before had Mother 'Possum seen anything like this. She played with the light for some time, making it go on and off and moving it so that the light would shine in different directions. It reminded her of that night they were rescuing Skunky when they had made noises to attract a beam of light first one way, then another.

When the light was off, she could see that the rest of the object was bright and shiny, about a foot long and big around as a full grown pawpaw, just such a thing as Mrs. Raccoon would like to put on her shelf of treasures.

Mentally marking the spot where it was, Mother 'Possum continued her search for new living quarters, but found nothing quite to her liking. Perhaps over at the Shining River where Beaver had been at work in the timber she could find something. But that could wait until tomorrow. Right now the prospect of presenting her friend with a gift was so pleasant that she started for the Grassy Meadow with the object tightly tucked in her pouch.

When Owl asked once again "Who? Whooo?" was passing through the woods, Mother 'Possum, being in a playful good humour, replied in a disguised voice, "The skunknappers, coming to take you to one of Skunky's far-off lands."

There was a swift, velvety flight of wings overhead. Mother 'Possum chuckled softly. Old Owl must feel as the rest of them did, that no matter how delightful Skunky could make some of those distant lands sound, really the Grassy Meadow, Rustling Brook, and Deep Forest were just about the best places on earth to live.

Mrs. Raccoon herself was just coming in from a nighttime stroll when Mother 'Possum arrived back at the hickory stump. They exchanged pleasantries about the beauty and fragrance of the moonlit night. Then Mother 'Possum brought out her present for Mrs. Raccoon, told where she had found it, and explained how with certain manipulations a light could be made to go on and off.

"It is a perfectly beautiful present," exclaimed Mrs. Raccoon, full of appreciation not only for the gift, but for the thoughtfulness of the giver.

"If you slide this little thing, a light will come on," said Mother 'Possum, pointing to a small sliding knob. She looked around for a stick, but Mrs. Raccoon, with her nimble fingers, was already manipulating the sliding device. In less than a minute she had the light on.

"Oh, my goodness!" she exclaimed, letting the thing go like a live coal. "It does give one a start, doesn't it?"

"I think it is harmless," said Mother 'Possum, slapping it smartly and kicking it to show that it wouldn't strike back.

Thus reassured, Mrs. Raccoon picked it up and soon found that she could turn the light on and off at will. She turned it up so that it shone in the doorway of her home and there, bright as two little stars, were Mr. Raccoon's eyes, staring down.

"Come on down," Mrs. Raccoon called. "It's not the hunters. Just me with a gift Mother 'Possum has brought."

She then turned the light in various other directions and saw the eyes of many of her other friends who had been attracted, but were keeping a safe distance.

"Come on out, everybody," she said, "and see what I have."

172

Skunky, Chipmunk, and Squirrel crept forward at Mrs. Raccoon's reassuring words.

"Whatever is it?" Chipmunk wanted to know.

"Blessed if I know," Mrs. Raccoon said. "Mother 'Possum found it up where the aeroplane fell."

"Has it got any words on it?" Mr. Raccoon asked.

By this time the moon had set, and there wasn't enough light to see. Mrs. Raccoon ran her delicate fingers over the object to see if she might feel any words. There seemed to be some kind of lid at the bottom. She twisted it several times and all at once it came off, the light went out, and out fell two small objects.

"Happened what did ever in the world?" demanded Chipmunk in his usual garbled way when scared or excited.

"I don't know," admitted Mrs. Raccoon, fearful that she had broken the fine new gift. She fingered the two small objects, smelled them, put them to her tongue, and batted them about with her feet, but nothing happened.

"Someone go get D.P.," Mr. Raccoon said. "He can tell us whether he's ever seen such a thing."

"And get Head Frog," added Mrs. Raccoon.

D.P. arrived first, being able to see a little better in the dark. But Head Frog was not far behind, although still blinking sleepily.

By the time they both arrived, it was beginning to get light. Head Frog peered closely at the objects and read aloud, "Flashlight battery. Guaranteed. 30p each, No. 950, Size D8."

Such shouts of victory went up from those gathered around the hickory stump that all creatures large and small, from a long distance around, came scampering, scurrying, scooting, flying, and hopping to see what was going on.

When they had all gathered, breakfastless and breathless with excitement, Mr. Raccoon asked them all to sit down in orderly rows, and then explained that by a happy circumstance they had come into possession of two flashlight batteries that were in good working condition. So it appeared they might be able to get the computer in working order.

The field mice, unable to contain themselves, shouted, "Light the lights! Push the buttons! Ask the question!"

This set off another resounding round of joy and jubilation which Mr. Raccoon, D.P., and Head Frog had a hard time stopping. Time after time they raised their hands for quiet only to have the blue jays start up, or all the little frogs make their half-grown croaks, or the 'possums stand on their heads and yell "Yippee" and "Yahoo" and "Yes sir."

But at last all was still. Mr. Raccoon, D.P., and Head Frog, who really hadn't been elected to any official position, but who nevertheless were regarded as being in charge, walked toward the brush-covered computer. They removed all the branches and weeds and grass that had been serving as camouflage. Everyone sighed with satisfaction at how beautiful the computer looked in the dawn's early light.

Mr. Raccoon opened the little door, removed two of the four batteries, and put the good ones in.

D.P. began to push all the buttons.

The excitement in the crowd grew until it was hard to tell whether it was only morning mist hanging over their heads or visible evidence of entrancement rising from their collective bodies.

One light, two lights, three lights, four lights—all came on with glittering brightness. Only three more to go. With his heart pounding against his ribs, D.P. pushed the fifth button. Nothing happened. He tried again. And again. The crowd, watching, leaned closer. D.P. went on to the sixth light. On it came. He went back to the fifth. Still no results.

Sighs and small whimperings began to arise from the crowd. Mr. Raccoon stepped forward. "Now just remain calm, folks," he said. "We probably have the wrong combination of batteries. We know some of them are not good. We've got to find the four good ones. So we'll try again." He opened the little door, took out the four batteries, and put them in a pile with the others. It was a mistake not to keep the two that were known to be good separate, but then batteries and their qualities and temperaments weren't everyday household concerns of those gathered around the computer.

"Would someone like to step forward and select the four batteries he feels might work?" asked Mr. Raccoon.

Mrs. Raccoon was first. When her set failed to work, Mother 'Possum tried, then Chuck and Chipmunk and Squirrel, Head Frog, seventeen blue jays, and forty-five meadow mice.

Spirits began to lower and tempers to rise. Everyone was getting hungry. By this time they'd thought they would have the answers to so many perplexing problems.

When Edward Meadow Mouse tried and it didn't work, he gave the computer a tiny kick with his hind leg, which he didn't care whether anyone saw or not.

"I think it is time for breakfast," said Mrs. Raccoon, who was sensing the rising dissatisfaction.

"More like time for dinner if you ask me," grumbled Chuck, who was usually such a good-natured fellow.

Instead of gathering their food and bringing it to share at the hickory stump, everyone went off to dine alone, and while they were thus alone each began to think of the first question he would ask the computer, for surely it would be in working order before nightfall.

One young 'possum thought he'd ask where there were some ripe persimmons, for he'd just rammed a ripe-looking one into his mouth and found it so sour he could hardly open his mouth to spit it out again.

Irene Meadow Mouse thought she might ask how she could make her hair look a little sleeker, her whiskers longer, her eyebrows more arched, for she was beginning to want to be noticed by someone, someone in particular—Edward Meadow Mouse.

Skunky went all the way over to the Shining River in search of his breakfast, which gave him plenty of time to think about the computer and its awesome properties, a thing he hadn't done much, he'd been so busy making up tales of the wonderful places he'd been up in the wild blue yonder. Suppose, he thought, someone should ask, "When am I going to die?" or "Will any of us freeze to death this winter?" or "Will the hunters come with their barking sticks and kill the raccoons, or

Squirrel, or Chuck?" And suppose the answer would come right back, "You, Skunky, will die on November 1st. Chipmunk will freeze to death this winter. Mrs. Raccoon will lose a leg in a trap."

Skunky shivered and decided quite definitely that he didn't want to know the answers to any of these questions. It was better to live with some unknowns. He hoped no one would ask anything like that. In fact, he felt that he must see to it that no one did. He ate hurriedly and went quickly back to the hickory stump, a plan formulating in his mind which might keep anyone from asking such questions.

Chuck went to the pawpaw patch for his lunch. He found the pawpaws to be sweet and succulent and remembered suddenly that it was always when the pawpaws were ripe that the folks of the Grassy Meadow, Deep Forest, and Rustling Brook held their annual Award Banquet. Funny, no one had mentioned it. He supposed that there had been too many other things to think about, but it had always been a rather pleasant affair and he hoped it wouldn't be dropped. Mother 'Possum might be eligible for the Award by finding the flashlight batteries. That is, if the thing ever worked.

When all had lunched and returned to the stump, the one hundred and thirteenth meadow mouse was working on his combination of batteries.

Skunky, putting into action the plan he had conceived, climbed onto the stump and began in his usual oratorical way, "Yes, sir, folks, there I was up there in the sky butterfly, ah, er, aeroplane if you will, and they dropped me off for a few hours in the Land of Fore-knowledge. Looked like a great place. Pretty trees. Green grass. Two suns, it had, so when one wasn't shining, the other one was. Rainbows all over the place. But I tell you, folks, it was awful. Not only awful, it was dreadful, horrible, frightful." Skunky used every terrifying word he could think of and finally got the response he wanted.

"Why?" demanded his listeners.

"Because—" Skunky paused, bowed his head as if it were too shocking to tell, then continued in a sober tone, "everyone knew ahead of time what was going to happen. I mean, *exactly* what was going to happen."

"What's so wrong with that?" asked D.P.

"Yeah. What's so wrong with that?" demanded half a dozen others.

"Well, one old fellow I met up there in the Land of Foreknowledge was sitting on his doorstep, staring out into space, looking so sad I felt compelled to ask, 'What's the matter, old fellow?' And he said, 'Next Thursday at two o'clock in the afternoon I'm going to be struck by lightning.' I asked him if he couldn't get away from where that was to happen if he knew when and where it was going to happen, and he said, 'Makes no difference where I'll be, it'll happen.' "

"Did it?" went up a chorus of questions.

"I didn't hang around to see. But walking on down the street, I came across some children playing hopscotch. Cutest little kids you have ever seen, clean and neat with shining hair. I watched for a while and noticed they didn't seem to be having any fun. So I asked why they weren't having any fun. They all looked at me as if I were stupid. Then, seeing I was a foreigner, one explained to me that they all knew who was going to win even before the game started."

"Did he?"

"He did."

Mrs. Raccoon shook her head sadly. D.P. closed his eyes in protest of such a predicament. Squirrel darted up a tree, sat on a branch, and frisked his tail most discontentedly.

It was plain to see that a querulous dissatisfaction was in the air, whereas only a few hours ago everyone had been dizzy with expectation and excitement.

Still the work on the computer went on. Such a thing ought not to just sit there if it could be made to work. Beaver, wet and glistening, dropped by to have a go at it. Six more blue jays tried, and the meadow mice continued—Marion, Paul, Louise, Christopher, Jane.

"My, oh my!" said Mrs. Raccoon, being quite dizzy with watching the batteries being shuffled in and out. "What everyone needs is a rest cure for his head."

22
Preparations Are Made for the Banquet

The days drifted by slowly as they are wont to do in autumn. The Deep Forest put on its gypsy clothes. Virginia creeper turned red and, with the bittersweet, festooned the hedgerow where soft breezes made their fairy music amongst the wild aster and joe-pye weed. But all the sweet, dreamy peace seemed out of step with the inhabitants. Work on the computer continued around the clock. One crisp morning when they had all gathered at the stump to see if anything new had happened, Head Frog, wishing to use some big words he'd thought of in the night, said, "An atmosphere of irritability, petulance, and perturbation is beginning to pervade the premises. That's I-R-R-I—" he began to spell, when D.P. interrupted in a peevish way, "Oh, who cares about the spelling."

Chuck chose this moment to climb onto the stump and indicate that he had something to say. Since Chuck didn't ordinarily do this, he got immediate, curious attention.

"Whereas," he began very legally. Liking the sound of it, he repeated, "Whereas the pawpaws are ripe and whereas there seems to be an atmosphere of interperbutation. . ." Chuck looked anxiously at Head Frog to see how well he had done with one of the big words. "And whereas it is this time of the year when we usually have the annual Deep Forest Award Banquet, I feel that it is high time to have that feast and presentation."

For a moment everyone stared blankly. How could they have forgotten such a thing as the Deep Forest Award Banquet! Then, all at once there was a great clapping, hooraying, and running around in happy circles. Forty-five of the meadow mice lined up, leaned backwards, and went down like a row of falling dominoes, although many of them were too young to know what the Deep Forest Award was. Neither did the young 'possums and some of the smaller frogs. Finally, when the noise of jubilation had died down, Timothy Meadow Mouse asked, "What is the Deep Forest Award?"

Chuck, who thought he'd had his say, motioned for Mr. Raccoon to mount the stump and explain.

"It's like this," Mr. Raccoon said. "Each year one person who in the opinion of the chairman has done the most useful and outstanding service, is selected to receive the Deep Forest, Rustling Brook, Grassy Meadow Award, called the Deep Forest Award for short. There is no plaque or scroll or metal; only the recognition by his friends that an outstanding deed has been done."

"It could be Mr. Raccoon himself," whispered one little meadow mouse to another. "I've heard he is very good about keeping the tin can tab openers and chewing gum wrappers picked up around here."

Chipmunk, who had overheard the meadow mice said, "Chuck was mighty efficient heading up the Disaster Committee when the storm came through last winter."

"Indeed he was," agreed Squirrel, who had also been listening.

"And there are lots of people who do great good

182

things and don't even know they do it and get no recognition," said Head Frog. "I was reading a piece of an old paper down at the dump the other day, and there was an article in it, front page, about a polecat putting out a fire in a crashed aeroplane with a spray from his body glands. That polecat will probably never know what good he did." Skunky gave the frog a peculiar smile.

"What's a polecat?" Squirrel wanted to know. "And what was he doing in an aeroplane?"

"Oh, maybe someone's pet or something. I didn't read the whole article," replied Head Frog.

"And there's Mrs. Raccoon who set Little Mocker's wing," suggested another meadow mouse. "And Mother 'Possum who found the batteries, which may someday work."

At this they all looked toward the computer, where still another meadow mouse was trying his combination to no avail.

"If the thing was working, we could ask and know in advance who was going to win the Award," said Head Frog, and then added, "That wouldn't be much fun."

"Who did we nominate to be this year's chairman of the Award?" asked Mr. Raccoon, scratching his head in an effort to remember.

No one seemed to recall that it was he or she.

"Suppose it was Rabbit?" Chuck said in a low, sad voice.

"Or maybe Beaver. He isn't here, is he?" Chipmunk queried. They all looked around for Beaver. Some said Beaver was working very hard these days getting his winter home ready, but they did seem to remember it was Beaver who was to be the chairman.

"I'll go get him," said D.P., starting off at a run.

Mr. Raccoon, still from his podium of the hickory

stump, said, "Now most of you are familiar with this event. We bring in the best food we can find, spread it banquet style, honour our outstanding citizen, and just have a jolly good time all around. So let's get at it!"

Before they began to scatter, Ruthie Meadow Mouse scampered to the top of the stump and tugged at Mr. Raccoon's leg, indicating she wished to say something, or rather have it said, because her little voice couldn't be heard very far.

Mr. Raccoon bent over to listen, straightened again, smiled, and said, "Ruthie says she thinks we ought to have some scrabbledobies."

All eyes turned toward Skunky.

Skunky blinked several times, put a finger to his temple, and tried to remember what he'd told them about scrabbledobies.

Chipmunk unwittingly came to Skunky's rescue, for he, like Ruthie and many others, had not forgotten the scrabbledobies. They liked the sound and the roll of the word on their tongues.

"You know," Chipmunk said. "It was in the land behind that cloud." He pointed in the direction of where the cloud had been that day. There wasn't any today, but that made no difference. "You said they take crushed hickory nuts and a dab of honey and that's as far as you got."

"Ah, yes," said Skunky, squinting his eyes as if to see into that distant land and remember. "You take hickory nuts and a dab of honey. But the honey can't be from just any old tree." He looked around to be sure he'd made a serious point. "It has to be from a tall, hollow sycamore tree. Then you add some butternuts, hazelnuts, sunflower seeds—lots of sunflower seeds—rosehips, and persimmon pulp. Mix it all together into little cakes, and you've got scrabbledobies."

184

An excited squawking broke out amongst the blue jays. When they quieted enough to make themselves intelligible, it was determined that they knew exactly where there was such a tree with honey in it.

"I'll get it," said Mrs. Raccoon, thinking of the little tin bucket on her treasure shelf and how suitable it would be for carrying the honey.

"We'll get the rosehips then," said the leader of the jays, and away they went in a big flurry of blue and white wings.

Chuck, who knew where ripe pawpaws were, started in that direction. Squirrel and Chipmunk called back over their shoulders that they would bring the nuts. Others scattered in various directions where they knew there were persimmons and sunflower seeds.

In her excitement Mrs. Raccoon started off toward the Shining River where a lot of sycamores grew without first determining just which sycamore it was that had honey. The blue jays had been negligent in their instructions about this, too. But it proved to be a minor matter because just as she was beginning to worry about the mistake, she met D.P. and Beaver making their way back to the Grassy Meadow.

"He's the chairman, all right," D.P. told Mrs. Raccoon.

"We're all out looking for banquet food," Mrs. Raccoon explained. "I'm going after some honey in a sycamore tree somewhere." She blushed and looked a little chagrined. "I forgot to ask the jays who knew about it just where the tree is."

"Cheer up," Beaver said. "I know it. When you get to the Shining River, you will see my lodge. Go to the seventh tree downstream on the right side and there, high up, you'll find the honey."

Mrs. Raccoon expressed her thanks and hurried

on. When she found the tree and climbed up to the opening, she asked very politely of the bees on duty if she might have a little honey.

There was a small meeting of the bees during which they decided they could spare a beenth of a bucket, which was a bee measurement. Upon inquiry, Mrs. Raccoon was pleased to learn that a beenth would almost fill the little tin bucket she had brought.

While the bees were getting the honey, Mrs. Raccoon sat on the edge of the doorway to their home and looked over the countryside. She thought that, if possible, this was a better view than the one from her own doorway. It was higher anyway, and one could see farther. There were distant ridges she had never seen before, blue and hazy now in the autumn mist. Then in front of these were nearer little hills where one could make out the red of sour gum, the crimson and gold of maple, the yellow of hickory. She thought that if Skunky were describing this land that lay in front of her, he might say that it looked as if rainbows had melted and run all over everything. Good old Skunky—he could very well be the winner of the Deep Forest Award by the way he kept them all entertained by his playacting and storytelling.

In front of the nearer hills, Mrs. Raccoon could see fields of browning corn, and then in front of that a field green with sprouting winter wheat. A small moving object at the farthest corner of the green field caught her eye. She watched it for a while, then turned her attention to the dozens of monarch butterflies going southward. The orange and black of their wings against the blue of the sky was a pleasing sight. A 'vee' of geese was winging along high over the butterflies. In between, two crows flip-flapped along, cawing a monotonous conversation.

When Mrs. Raccoon looked at the green field

again, she noted that the small moving object was closer than before. Still, she could not make out what it was. It seemed to stop and rest a while, then move on again, slower and slower each time as if very tired.

When the bees indicated they had the bucket filled, Mrs. Raccoon thanked them kindly and hung the bucket on a small branch to have another look at the beautiful scenery before starting home. Autumn, she thought, was just as sweet as spring with its warmth and lazy sunshine. There was faint wood smoke instead of honeysuckle in the air. The fields were singing with crickets instead of meadowlarks, and a sort of peaceful waiting hung over the countryside.

She looked once more at the object moving across the green wheat field. Her heart leaped. Little jiggles of excitement started somewhere near the end of her seven-ringed tail and made their way up along her spine, tickled her ribs, shook her fingers, chattered her teeth. What she saw was a rabbit. Not just any rabbit, she thought, but maybe Rabbit of Grassy Meadow!

Down the sycamore tree she went, through the woods, over logs, hopping, skipping, jumping, her tail standing straight out behind.

"What's up?" shouted those who saw her, dropping nuts, persimmons, and sunflower seeds to follow.

Mrs. Raccoon did not stop to explain, but just told them all to follow her, lickety-split!

She stumbled over Turtle, and thinking it might be hours before Turtle could get to the Stump, picked him up, and carried him under her arm.

Many had already returned with their banquet food, and before Mrs. Raccoon could get her breath to tell what she had seen, all the others were back.

"Rab-rabb-rabbit!" she said, panting for breath. "I th-thi-think he's co-coming." She pointed, as usual, with all five fingers at once, and several started out in five different directions before they realized their mistake.

"Tha-that-thataway," said Mrs. Raccoon making a fist this time and pointing in the direction of the green wheat field.

23

The Homecoming of Rabbit and Little Mocker

Little Mocker and Rabbit had made good progress since the day they started toward the distant outline of the Deep Forest, but it was much further away than they had realized.

With his newfound flying ability, Little Mocker felt that he could easily have made it in one day, but he was really grateful when from time to time Rabbit called up to him that he couldn't go another step without stopping to catch his breath.

Rabbit had grown awfully thin, for with their haste to get home they hadn't had much time to eat. Also, a briar had scratched him across the nose, a front foot was sore and swollen, and with the missing hunks of fur he was a scraggly looking sight.

"Perhaps we'd better make camp and wait around here a week or two," Little Mocker suggested one day, although his own heart was bursting inside with little secret thrills that kept saying, "Home, home, home."

"Only long enough for ten bites of clover," Rabbit replied, already having consumed five, the dew from which, mingled with the early sunshine, was making rainbows in his whiskers. The thought of his own comfortable fuzz-lined bed in the hedgerow bordering the Grassy Meadow was overpoweringly strong. He knew that he was weak and sore and stiff and must present a frightful appearance, but felt that unless he got home he would never again be strong.

On the fourth day after their aimless wanderings had ceased and they had started in the right direction, Little Mocker, flying ahead, glimpsed the white oak home of Mr. and Mrs. Raccoon. He descended immediately to tell Rabbit the good news.

"I thought I recognized these fields. I know where I am now, Little Mocker. If you want to go on ahead, I won't be far behind."

"Nonsense! We will go home together," said Little Mocker, flying back up to travel the airways, but at the same time keeping an eye on his earthbound friend to see that he did know where he was going.

On and on Rabbit went, across the green wheat field, slowly, painfully, sustained by the thought of how Mrs. Raccoon would tend to his sore foot. Chipmunk would make him a sweet green salad. Skunky would— Skunky! He wondered if Skunky had been able to get out of that trap! He crossed the Rustling Brook and was making his way through the Grassy Meadow when he heard voices raised in gladness and shouting. "Here comes Rabbit! Rabbit! Rabbit! Here comes Rabbit!"

Soon Rabbit felt himself being carried along on a pack-saddle formed by the crossed, clasped arms of Mr. and Mrs. Raccoon. Others ran alongside, picking burs and prickles from his fur and speaking loving words of gladness and joy and "Where, oh where had he been? Was he well? Did Dog hurt him?"

The frogs hopped up and down stiff-legged. The meadow mice turned triple somersaults. The 'possums caught hold of each other's tails and ran around and around in dizzy circles. Skunky, walking backwards in front of Rabbit, stumbling, falling, getting up again, tried to think of all the thankful words he knew to let Rabbit know how particularly glad he was to see him alive and home again.

Rabbit tried to be heard above the noise of jubilation. "Little Mocker!" he shouted and pointed upward to where Little Mocker was now perched on a branch of the big white oak. But his friends paid little attention to the gesture. Some who did looked up only to see a strange bird and thought him a part of the southerly migration.

Mrs. Raccoon, who had heard, said, "No, Rabbit, Little Mocker has never returned. But you are here, dear friend. Home at last. Safe and sound."

"But that's him," Rabbit protested, becoming embarrassed that so much was being made over his return and no one noticing Little Mocker at all. He looked up at his friend in dismay and saw Little Mocker make a slight motion to keep silent about his presence. Perplexed and bewildered, but respecting Little Mocker's wishes, Rabbit did so.

Chipmunk brought a sweet green salad. Mrs. Raccoon brought her freshly laundered Flower Garden quilt and puffed it up around Rabbit. The noise of the glad reunion went on and on, with little made-up songs, marches, and every kind of demonstration the folks of the Grassy Meadow, Deep Forest, and Rustling Brook could think of.

"Now what we will have to do," said Mr. Raccoon, "is all be quiet and let Rabbit tell about his adventures."

So Rabbit, refreshed by the food and comforted by the softness of the quilt, told about how he had been chased by Dog, shot in the leg, and chased some more by Dog until he landed in the dreaded Next County. He saw the chills and quivers that ran through his audience, heard the chattering of teeth. "I lay for hours beneath a rock pile with a strange and ferocious creature just waiting for me to come out. If it hadn't been for a friend—" Rabbit glanced up, and again Little Mocker motioned for silence.

"A friend in the Next County?" went up simultaneous questions of disbelief.

"Well, he wasn't exactly from the Next County. Anyway, if it hadn't been for this friend, I probably wouldn't be here today."

At this point Little Mocker began a soft little song to accompany the rest of Rabbit's story. It was hardly noticeable at first, but grew more eloquent as Rabbit went on. It was as if they had been practising for a long time, so well was the song suited for the words. When Rabbit told of the morning he and his friend had decided to strike out in some direction in hope of getting out of the Next County, there was sprightly, determined march time in the notes. When he told of their mode of travel, ricket-rackety piggyback, on account of the fact that his friend was wounded too, there was a mixture of jig time, off notes, and intermittent tones of defeat, overcome gradually by sweet sounds of victory and perfect timing.

"And then one day we rounded a corner and there was a bear!" said Rabbit.

At this, Little Mocker gave such a comical series of alarm notes that several of the citizens glanced up to have a closer look at this bird who seemed to have such an astounding assortment of indescribable little runs, trills, and cadenzas all out of proportion to his size and who seemed to know by some strange communication just what was going on below.

By this time, Rabbit himself had caught on to what Little Mocker was doing, so he left out no detail. "Then came a day we realized we were out of the Next County," he went on. Here he paused a long time, and the silence was filled with the sweetest song ever heard in the Grassy Meadow. It was sunlight and rainbows and moonbeams and clover and soft breezes all captured and melted into a liquid run of glad piping that held the listeners transfixed. They were strangely moved as if they had listened to music that came from somewhere beyond the bird's throat, beyond the treetops, up, up to the realms of the Keeper of All Creatures Himself.

When the music died down to a mere whisper, Rabbit said, "And so, I am here." He looked up at Little Mocker with such pleading in his eyes that Little Mocker knew it was time to identify himself. As if he had expressly exploded himself with song, he flurried down from the tree, a ball of ruffled grey feathers, to fall at Mrs. Raccoon's feet with a small thud and mock collapse. "Cheep, cheep, cheep," he went.

Mrs. Raccoon raised her hands in alarm and said, "Oh my." She rolled the bird over, tried to open its eyes, and then repeated, "Oh my. Head Frog, I do believe it needs resuscitation."

Head Frog stepped forward, swelling with importance. He opened the bird's beak and attempted to breathe into its mouth. At this the bird's eyes flew open. It "Cheep, cheep, cheeped" madly and scrabbled about first this way, then that, making a rickety figure eight, a figure four, a figure six, and a little *i*, pecking a dot over it.

Everyone seemed to have remembered going through all this before. They stood dazed and confused, made helpless little motions as if they had once known what to do next, but had forgotten.

Little Mocker straightened himself, shook his feathers, and said, "Hello, Mrs. Raccoon, Mr. Raccoon, Skunky, Chipmunk, Chuck, Squirrel, meadow mice, frogs." Round the circle he went, calling them by name, which only confounded the gathering more. How could this strange bird know them?

It was Mrs. Raccoon who recovered first. With a glad cry she shouted, "It is Little Mocker. Little Mocker grown up!"

The joyous commotion of the glad reunion was repeated all over again, with each one thinking up some new and different way to express his delight. The meadow mice, standing on each other's shoulders, built the tallest pyramid they'd ever made. The blue jays dipped and looped and made most complicated patterns in the air. Mother 'Possum, absolutely overcome, swooned and missed a little of the rejoicing. D.P. stood on his forelegs, his hind legs in the air, and whipped his tail around and around so fast it created a miniature whirlwind.

In the midst of all the gaiety, Lauren Meadow Mouse, whose turn it had been at the combination of batteries for the Little Toy Computer, came running into the crowd, shouting as loud as she could, "All the lights are lit. All the lights are lit!" No one heard her, so she climbed right up Mr. Raccoon's shoulder and shouted into his ear, "All the lights are lit on the Little Toy Computer."

24

The Brass Trimmed Box Gives Its Answer

Mr. Raccoon clapped loudly for silence. "Friends," he began in a voice that denoted something of great import was to be announced. "Friends, as if we have not had enough good news this day, Lauren Meadow Mouse has just this moment told me that all the lights are now lit on the Little Toy Computer."

A ripple of gasps and softly spoken "Oh me's" and "Oh my's" passed over the crowd. Everyone sat down quickly. Now that the moment had actually arrived for answers to any and all questions, no one was quite ready for his all-important first one. A few remembered about the land Skunky had told of where everyone knew ahead of time what was going to happen, but the memory was quickly put aside. Why would such a wonderful computer be invented if it were not to be used?

Rabbit and Little Mocker stared at each other blankly. What new thing must have happened in their absence to cause such a solemn and awesome attitude? Seeing their expression, Mr. Raccoon quickly explained all about the Little Tiny Computer and its purported capabilities, how they had worked nearly all summer trying to find batteries and then the right combination of workable ones. "I'm sure that our first questions, should we have gotten it to work sooner, were going to be 'Where are Rabbit and Little Mocker?' But now that you are here, whoever asks the first question will have to think of something different."

"Do we have to tell what we ask?" inquired Irene Meadow Mouse, blushing furiously.

"No," replied Mr. Raccoon. "Unless, of course, it is something that will affect the whole community such as, Will the forest catch on fire this autumn? Will the river flood? Where will traps be set?' and so forth."

"Who goes first?" asked Chipmunk, voicing the question that was on everyone's mind.

"Well, in honour of our two returning friends, I think we should let them go first," suggested Mr. Raccoon.

A shout of agreement went up from the crowd.

"We don't know how it works," protested Rabbit, thinking this a huge honour, but also a huge responsibility.

"I'll show you," said Head Frog. "Come this way." He led Rabbit and Little Mocker to where the Little Toy Computer stood, its brass corners gleaming, its lights all shining brightly.

"See this button?" Head Frog asked.

Little Mocker and Rabbit nodded, indicating they did.

"This is the last button to push after all the lights are lit. Push it in, ask a question, and Little Toy Computer will answer. Understand?"

Again Little Mocker and Rabbit nodded affirmatively.

Head Frog returned to the crowd to await the result.

Little Mocker and Rabbit looked at each other for a long time. A shiver of excitement rippled down Rabbit's back. Little Mocker fluffed his feathers to calm himself, then said, in an attempt to help the moment,

196

"Well, if it answers any and all questions, we shouldn't be too scared. Our first question might be, 'What should we ask of you, Little Toy Computer?' "

"It might break down after the first question," Rabbit purposed. "And we wouldn't have gained anything."

They looked at each other for another long time, each thinking of the experiences they'd had the past summer, of the happy homecoming, of the difference in the folks here at home and those in the Next County.

At last Rabbit spoke. "I've been thinking of the Next County," he began.

"Of those who live there?" Little Mocker asked eagerly, as if Rabbit was touching on his own thoughts.

"Exactly," Rabbit said. "Of how different they are."

"And what makes the difference?" added Little Mocker.

It seemed as if their thoughts were as synchronized as their earlier performance of song and story.

"Why, yes, indeed!" replied Rabbit, agreeably surprised that Little Mocker seemed to be reading his mind.

"And if we knew what made the difference, how we could help those miserable creatures?" continued Little Mocker.

"Little Mocker, you have put it exactly."

Together they worked on their questions until they had every word in place. Then they pushed the final button, and Rabbit asked in a clear strong voice, "What is there here among the neighbours of the Grassy Meadow, Deep Forest, and Shining River that is lacking in the Next County?" They sat back and listened with a passionate intentness.

Deep inside the Little Toy Computer came some small clickings and clackings, brushings and grindings.

And when everything seemed to have fallen in place, a voice said distinctly, "Love." This was followed by a few more little raspings, a final click, and all lights went out.

Little Mocker and Rabbit sat silent for a long time, spellbound. They looked at each other, then looked away as if the moment was too profound for them to handle. Each in turn was caught up in a trembling which was but visible evidence of the unspeakable joy and rapturous delight that flooded their bodies when the full import of what had happened penetrated the deepest recesses of their minds. *An answer to everything!* And such a *right* answer, they thought.

Eventually, when Little Mocker felt he had enough control of himself to proceed, and to test the computer again, he said, "I'm ready with another question."

Rabbit, still too overcome to speak, only nodded.

Little Mocker pushed the buttons, watched all the lights come on, paused briefly, then pushed the final button and asked, "How can we help the folks in the Next County?"

There were the same noises as before. Rabbit extended his ears to full measure. Little Mocker cocked his head, the better to hear, and back came the answer, "Love."

The two friends looked at each other again, this time a bit disconcerted. Love those horrible creatures? How could they? They had thought the Little Toy Computer might give instructions concerning severe chastisements and incarcerations. Their brows furrowed. Little Mocker scratched the ground petutantly. Rabbit's ears drooped. His whiskers stood out stiff and bristly.

They heard sounds of impatience from outside

and knew the others were anxious to get at the computer with their questions. In silence they returned to the crowd.

"Well?" went up a questioning chorus. "Did it answer?"

"It did," said Rabbit.

"Yes, it did," agreed Little Mocker.

"What did you ask? What did it answer?" everyone wanted to know.

Mr. Raccoon, seeing the mixed emotions on Little Mocker's and Rabbit's faces, clapped for attention and reminded that no one need tell what he asked or what the answer was if he didn't want to.

Attention was turned to who should go next.

"Since Mrs. Raccoon found the computer, I feel she should have that privilege," said D.P.

Mrs. Raccoon protested, saying that it was D.P. himself and Head Frog and all the frogs and meadow mice who got the computer out of the dump pile, so maybe they ought to draw straws.

"Draw straws!" exclaimed Mother 'Possum. "With three hundred and fifty meadow mice, plus all the rest of us? Fifty of us could have our questions asked before all the straws were drawn. No, I say let Mrs. Raccoon go next."

There was agreement, so Mrs. Raccoon indeed went next.

Since she had already done much thinking about whether it would be good to know the answer to everything, it did not take long for her to ask, "Is it good to know all the answers?" When the answer came back, "Love," she was somewhat stunned, since she had been expecting a simple "yes" or "no." She would like to have asked the question again, be a bit more specific, but knowing others were waiting, she turned and joined the crowd, with only a slight look of puzzlement on her face.

"Is it still working?" D.P. wanted to know.

"Still working," replied Mrs. Raccoon, although she knew she would have to study the answer for a while to see where it fitted her question.

Head Frog was next to go. Knowing about such elementary grammatical things as commas and conjunctions, he had figured out a way he might ask two questions for the push of one. So he asked, "Where did Skunky go this summer when we thought him lost, and how does he manage to tell things in such a way that we all more than halfway believe everything he says, although we don't really think he means us to?" The question turned out to be much longer than Head Frog had intended. While all the little clickings and raspings were going on, preliminary to the answer, he feared the computer might say, "Please repeat," or "Your sentence is too long. Please condense." It really wasn't a very profound question, but there would be plenty of time later to get down to more philosophical ones. When the answer came back, "Love," he winked and blinked and choked on a croak. He went back outside, squatted down, and winked and blinked some more.

D.P. was next. Remembering how long they had looked for workable batteries, he asked right off, "How long are these batteries going to work in you?" When he heard the answer, "Love," he thought he hadn't made himself clear and although he knew it was somewhat of an unspoken agreement that each one should have only one question until everybody had a turn, he pushed all the buttons and asked the same question again. And again. And again. He even tried another question. And another. And another.

He shook the Little Toy Computer, and rapped it smartly with his tail. But as constant as daylight following darkness, the same answer came, "Love. Love. Love."

D.P. was annoyed and disappointed. They had worked so hard and long to get the computer to work, and now it was stuck on "Love." Maybe, he thought, it wasn't speaking in the universal language of the Grassy Meadow, Deep Forest, and Rustling Brook. Maybe "love" in computer language meant "humbug" or "fool!" D.P. hit his forehead with his fist as if to jar loose anything that was causing a malfunction of his brains, then began laying out facts on his fingers. Head Frog had read the instructions on the computer, and they had worked. So the language the computer used must be the same language as the instructions that made it work. Therefore, love must be love in any language. Oh, it was all too much for D.P.'s head. It began to ache terribly. He stumbled back out to the crowd, holding his head with both hands.

"What's the matter, D.P.?" asked Mrs. Raccoon, who saw his misery.

"What's the matter?" repeated D.P. crossly. "That thing has only one answer."

"Only one answer!" demanded a group of meadow mice who had been busy organizing hundreds of questions amongst themselves so they'd know where to get food supplies this coming winter and build the coziest homes that wouldn't be iced in or snowed under.,

"That's right," D.P. said. "Only one answer." He kicked the ground and picked up an oak ball and threw it far as he could.

Head Frog stopped his choked croaking, winking, and blinking and hopped up close. "Was that answer 'Love'?" he asked.

"Yes, that answer was 'love,'" said D.P., switching his tail angrily, which clearly showed that the answer hadn't suited his question.

201

"It was my answer too," Mrs. Raccoon said.

"And ours," said Rabbit and Little Mocker.

Where only a few minutes before there had been sounds of merriment, now there was only sullen silence. They had been cheated, made fools of. Dreams of henceforth untroubled lives vanished like smoke in a quick wind. All the 'possums curled up and sulked. Squirrel ran up a tree and chattered in a most irritating manner. Chipmunk lay down, kicked his four feet in the air, and wailed. Beaver began gnawing at the foot of the big white oak tree until Mr. Raccoon saw what he was doing and gave him a swift cuff with his hand, which sent Beaver rolling.

Rabbit and Little Mocker, for whom the answer "love" had made good sense, began trying to bring order out of the chaos. Little Mocker flew to a branch of the white oak and began singing. The compellingly sweet music imposed its will on those below. Noises of discontent began to die down. Mr. Raccoon apologized to Beaver, and Beaver said he was sorry, he just wasn't thinking what he was doing. Chipmunk kicked with only three feet, then two, then one, and finally righted himself.

Rabbit hopped around from first one to another, telling all over again how good it was to be back home in the Grassy Meadow. He complimented the meadow mice on the perfection of their pyramids, told Mother 'Possum of a hollow tree over by the wheat field that would make a good home, marveled at the growth of the little 'possums who had opened their eyes and got lively again, congratulated Head Frog for his keeping abreast of the written language. In and out he went, inquiring of health and happenings and speaking of good times ahead, until peace and order was restored.

Then, into the semiquietness came a buzzing sound, growing louder and louder.

"A whirlwind," whispered Chipmunk.

"A fire," quavered Chuck.

"A chainsaw come to cut down the forest," predicted Skunky.

The buzzing sound came right over the top of the white oak tree, paused, and started to descend.

Mrs. Raccoon, who had been looking very thoughtful ever since learning of the computer's one answer, was the first to get a glimpse of what it was and squealed with delight, "It's my honey. I forgot my honey!"

The others looked upward to see a swarm of bees holding onto a length of grapevine at the end of which dangled Mrs. Raccoon's little tin bucket.

With an uncommon show of dexterity, the bees lowered the bucket until it rested in the center of the old hickory stump.

"Thank you. Thank you," Mrs. Raccoon called up to the bees. "Won't you come and share our feast?" But the bees, after dipping their wings in acknowledgment of the thanks, flew away, and everyone understood that bees were very busy at this time of the year, sealing and waxing and so forth.

It was Mrs. Raccoon's word "feast" that swept away the last remnants of disappointment with the Little Toy Computer and its one answer to everything.

"Scrabbledobies!" shouted Ruthie Meadow Mouse, suddenly remembering the delectable delicacy Skunky had described. "We's gonna have scrabbledobies!"

"And grapes and nuts and sunflower seeds and green salads and the Deep Forest Award!" added many others.

Of course Little Mocker and Rabbit had to be told about the scrabbledobies and where Skunky had got the recipe and that they had all been in the process of gathering the ingredients when Little Mocker and Rabbit had appeared, and then had come the surprise of the computer being made to work after weeks and weeks of trials with the batteries.

"My oh my, what a happening day!" said Chuck, who just loved any manner of excitement.

Skunky, realizing that there was no way out of making scrabbledobies, began to stall for time. He looked over the supplies that had been brought and said, "It seems to me that we don't have nearly enough nuts and persimmons and sunflower seeds."

"We left ours out in the woods when we learned Rabbit was coming," said several, while others eagerly volunteered to get more. And away they went.

25
The Deep Forest Award

D.P. hurried off to the dump pile. Just yesterday, after the dumping of a new load of miscellaneous items, he had recovered a half round of cheese. It was very old and hard, just the way he liked it. He had hoped to nibble on it all winter when things got cold and tough, but now he wished to share it with his friends. Also, he felt that he should look around for an old dishpan in which to mix the scrabbledobies.

As he made his way over logs and leaves and heaps and hummocks, his thoughts went back to the foolish answer the computer had given when he had asked how long the batteries would last. Of course if the computer had given some sensible answer like, "One hour," or "Ten minutes," he could just imagine the great scramble that would have resulted as everyone tried to have his turn at the computer before it expired. Why, lifelong enemies could have been made. As it was, even without answers to many pressing questions, they all got along rather nicely. In fact, a little more than nicely. Look at the way Mrs. Raccoon took care of everybody when they were hurt, and the way Rabbit and Little Mocker had teamed up to get back home from the terrible Next County, and the way Rabbit had gone off in the first place, leading Dog away so they could rescue Skunky.

D.P.'s brow furrowed with laboured thinking. Maybe there was something to this one and only answer the computer gave; something more than met the eye, the brain, or whatever it was the answer met. Someday, when he had more time, he'd really sit down and think it through, but right now there was the cheese and dishpan to think about.

Head Frog marshalled all the lesser frogs and hopped off to the Rustling Brook, where they had been in the process of gathering watercress when news of Rabbit's coming had been shouted out. He plunged into and out of the clear cool water several times, hoping to clear his mind so it could understand and accept the answer the computer had given him. His question about where Skunky had gone this summer wasn't too terribly important. It was just a kind of curiosity satisfier until he could think of something better. But the answer! Was it in any way appropriate? Could it in some subtle, mysterious, roundabout way be a proper answer?

In a few minutes Head Frog began to have new and inspiring thoughts. "Old Skunky," he murmured, and smiled tolerantly. He really enjoyed Skunky's dramatic tales and, come to think of it, it seemed as if they always came at a time when folks needed cheering, or needed to get their minds off troublesome things. Maybe Skunky planned it that way. In that case, he was being kind. No, more than kind. One might say he was showing love. *Love!* A peculiar little ripple made its way down Head Frog's back. He began to smile little short smiles which soon grew into middle-sized smiles, and then such a great big smile it seemed the corners of his mouth were almost touching somewhere on top of his head. He wondered—he just wondered—if the computer might be smarter than any of them thought. Surely it was trying to say that Skunky's motive for telling about his "travels" was *love*. Someday he'd suggest to his friends that the one answer the computer gave was—he tried to think of some big word. Plunging into and out of the water several more times, he finally came up with the word, *all-encompassing*. "That's A-L-L-E-N-C-O-M-P-A-S-S-I-N-G," he spelled aloud, practising.

"Does that mean we've got enough? asked a lesser frog, pointing to the pile of watercress they had gathered.

"No. Yes. No. That is, it doesn't mean you've got enough. But yes, you have enough," replied Head Frog.

The lesser frogs winked and blinked. Really, it was sometimes awfully hard to understand Head Frog, but then it was hard to keep up with one who could read and spell so well. Perhaps they'd learn someday, but now there was the banquet and the Award and fun and games.

Although Rabbit and Little Mocker had offered to go out and bring in their share of food for the feast, the others had insisted they stay right there on the Flower Garden quilt and rest.

"In fact," said Mrs. Raccoon, "you'll have time for a little nap."

So Rabbit closed his eyes, and Little Mocker tucked his head beneath his wing, but neither of them could sleep. The answer the computer had given them had been so mysteriously forceful that whether or not it was the same answer to every question, it was *their* answer, *their* marching orders!

"We've got to go back," said Rabbit after a while.

"To the Next County?" said Little Mocker, bringing his head from beneath his wing. It was more of a statement than a question.

"To the Next County," said Rabbit. And then, as if to reinforce it, he said, "Come next spring, we've got to go back to the Next County and teach them the ways of love, clean up that river and forest floor, stop that fighting, and tell them of the Keeper."

A silence stretched between them as each thought of the desperate times they'd had there and how, if they went back, they could possibly begin to show that love made such a difference in living conditions and general all-around happiness.

Finally Rabbit broke the stillness. "We've got to try. We'll take a whole delegation," he planned. "Each one will have some good idea."

"Mr. and Mrs. Raccoon and the 'Possums and Skunky and Chuck, and Beaver—" Little Mocker started listing.

"Any and all who want to go. We've just got to try," said Rabbit.

"It seems to me, Rabbit," said Little Mocker, smiling slyly, "that we've been pretty successful at things we set our minds to. A little wobbly at first, maybe. But in the end, pretty successful."

Rabbit nodded, smiled, winked, and nodded again, his long ears expressing very eloquently his belief that they could indeed bring order out of the chaos of the Next County if they employed the answer the computer had given them.

Mrs. Raccoon, after seeing that Rabbit and Little Mocker were comfortably tucked about with her puffy quilt, climbed to her home in the big white oak. There, sitting in the doorway, looking out over the dearly loved Grassy Meadow, hedgerow, and Rustling Brook, bridged now with late golden sunshine, she let her thoughts nibble at the answer the computer had given to her question about whether it was good to know all the answers to everything. The answer, "love," had been given so promptly and joyfully, so full of assurance, that she had to believe that it must have been fitting, although at the moment it hadn't seemed so. Had Man, who made the Little Toy Computer (because Man made almost everything that eventually landed in the dump pile), found somewhere along the line that love was a magic answer to everything? If the computer answered "love" when asked if a fire would sweep the forest next week, did it mean that the Keeper of All Creatures loved them so much he wanted to spare them this specific foreknowledge? And if the disaster did befall, was it love of creature for creature that made it bearable, made them look out and care for one another? Did it mean that if a person worked love into all situations, not only when things were going well, but when situations were desperate, that right actions and reactions would be assured? If Man had found this out, did he follow it in everyday living? Or had he, in the daily cares of living, dumped it by the wayside somewhere just as the Little Toy Computer had been dumped?

Beginning at the far corner of the hedgerow, Mrs. Raccoon let her eyes travel slowly along, enjoying old memories of things that had happened in the plum thicket and the persimmon patch. She watched her friends and neighbours returning with their contributions for the banquet. There was Chuck with an armload of pawpaws; a long procession of meadow mice bearing seeds; Chipmunk and Squirrel with nuts; Beaver, Mr. Raccoon, and all the 'possums with bunches of grapes; D.P. struggling up through the woods with what looked like a round of cheese and a pan about ten times bigger than he was.

The lowering sun was making golden threads of long floating spiderwebs. Mrs. Raccoon watched them lodge on the tree branches, wild asters, stumps, brambles, and briars. They seemed to be weaving an intricate protective golden web around them all. And inside the web was a roseate glow from end-of-day sunshine, livened by shouts of merriment from those beginning to mix the scrabbledobies, those arranging the pawpaws in attractive little stacks, and those just talking over the happenings of the day. She looked in the direction of the now abandoned and uncovered computer. Rays from the setting sun caught and hung on the brass corners. One corner seemed to send a special red-gold beam right up to where she was sitting. No matter which way she turned her head it was there, almost as if it had her trapped. She knew, of course, that she could go back further into the room, or even down the tree and get out of it, but she rather liked its warmth and glow and the airy, graceful feeling of being held up by a sunbeam that had no substance.

Such a feeling reminded Mrs. Raccoon of the time she had tried so hard to explain the Keeper of All Creatures to Little Mocker; how He did not keep anyone harshly chained, but that His chain, if anything, was more like warm sunbeams linking His creatures together.

At that moment the sunbeam from the computer almost blinded her. Then, suddenly it went away. No matter how she turned, twisted, or stretched, she could not get it back. She looked at the computer in a thoughtful, puzzled sort of way. Of course, she could see that shadows were gathering down below, but it was almost as if the computer had given her a big parting wink.

From somewhere down deep inside, a thought began to take shape. She remembered she had also told Little Mocker that although no one ever saw the Keeper, she sometimes felt as if she had seen where He had just been. She grappled mightily with the thought to bring it into focus and form. It grew and grew, like a soft, white, glowing light, until it stood clear and shiny in her mind.

Mrs. Raccoon trembled with mingled awe and reverence. She looked again at the computer. Her heart swelled. Her eyes gleamed. "Surely I've seen where the Keeper has just been, and He left a message!" she whispered. Quickly she left her doorway and descended the trunk of the white oak so hurriedly she landed upside down. But, no matter—she must tell the others.

"Yes sir, there I was, folks, up there in Scrabbledobie Land," Skunky was saying, beginning still another tale.

"Wait, wait," Mrs. Raccoon said, coming into the circle and speaking in a voice that brought them all to quick attention.

They gathered around her respectfully.

"Most of you have heard the answer the computer has given, and the rest have heard about it. I, for one, think it makes sense, even though it is always the same answer, 'Love.' "

"That's L-O-V-E," spelled Head Frog, who felt so good about everything he simply couldn't keep still.

"L-O-V-E," everyone echoed in voices that ranged three notes over two octaves.

"Furthermore," Mrs. Raccoon continued, "I think it is the Keeper who has just used the computer to commune with us, and 'Love' is His great overall message."

At this all heads bowed. Little fingers intertwined. Eyes closed. Paws crossed. A great silence descended; a silence in which each creature, however dim his sense of the Keeper might be, knew of His presence and gave thanks. Rabbit, sitting next to Little Mocker and feeling him tremble so, reached over and placed a loving paw on his back.

It was some time before they could let go of this moment. Never did they forget it.

When the sun had sunk behind the hedgerow, leaving a glorious afterglow in the sky, Skunky began again, "Yes sir, there I was in Scrabbledobie Land when they insisted that I make some of their national tidbits. They placed me on a marble table." Skunky looked around for a marble table and, as if he had luckily found one, climbed onto the stump. "They handed me a pan made of pure gold."

D.P. handed up the chipped blue iron pan.

"And everyone marched by in procession, dropping in the things that made for scrabbledobies," Skunky instructed.

At this the three hundred and fifty-six meadow mice marched by, two abreast, and dropped in their seeds. Some who couldn't find sunflower seeds dropped in millet, timothy, or bluegrass seeds. Chuck dropped in some seeded pawpaws. Others came with their persimmon pulp.

"Then round and round, over, in and out and through, I mixed it with a golden spoon." Skunky looked up to indicate he had no golden spoon.

Mr. Raccoon was quick to supply a stout hickory stick.

"Thicker and thicker it got," said Skunky, breathing hard as he mixed the sweet concoction. "Until—until—at last—at last," he huffed and puffed—"until at last, it was ready to eat!" He waved the hickory stick in victory, licked it clean, closed his eyes, and smacked his lips to indicate that this truly was food to be found only in some magic land.

The meadow mice jumped up and down with impatience to get at the scrabbledobies.

Never before and probably never since has there been such a picnic around the old hickory stump. The stomachs of the meadow mice grew rounder and rounder and puffed out like miniature balloons. For once in their lives, the 'possums declared they had enough persimmons. Head Frog promised to write down the recipe for the scrabbledobies and hide it under some rock for future generations, for everyone declared it the most scrumpsidotious delicacy they'd ever tasted. D.P. suggested that if he could find a proper file, the recipe might even be chiseled into some flat rock where it would last and last, and someday might become a sort of lost legend. Folks in years to come might occupy themselves when walking and picnicking in the woods by scraping off lichens and moss from old rocks, bluffs, ledges, and cave sides in search of the lost recipe.

By the time the moon came up to cast a silver light on everything, every last berry, nut, rosehip, green sal-

213

ad, and scrabbledobie cake had been consumed and all things tidied and put in order. While others were arranging themselves in neat circles around the stump, Beaver, in honour of his chairmanship, slipped off to groom himself. He parted his dark brown fur in the middle from the end of his nose to the base of his tail, slicked it down, made sure his fingernails were clean and that his whiskers were free of all signs of food. Returning to the circle of friends, he mounted the stump and made a nice speech about the happenings of the past year. He was interrupted often by applause as he mentioned the efforts of first one, then another who had made the community a better place in which to live. He recognized those who had previously won the Award, which brought even louder applause.

"And now comes the time for this year's Award," said Beaver, pausing so as to get full attention. "As you all know, there is no greater deed than that of one person risking his life for another. Perhaps we have all done this in small, unseen, unnoticed ways from time to time, but last spring Rabbit did it in a very noble way when, in the face of grave danger to himself, he led Dog away so we could rescue Skunky. So I hereby this day proclaim dear fearless Rabbit this year's winner of the Deep Forest Award."

A great shout of approval went up, and Rabbit felt himself being lifted onto the shoulders of several friends and paraded around the stump. Little Mocker sang the sprightliest march tune anyone had ever heard as he dipped and swayed and looped the loop.

There was no use in Rabbit's protesting that he hadn't done any more to deserve the Award than any of the others. Every time he started to, they shouted him down and began singing, "For he's a fearless good Rabbit." At last he managed a simple, "Thank you." And then, remembering a thought he'd had back in the Next County when he had been in such desperate straits, he added, "I love every one of you."

Even though the hour was late, a number of meadow mice organized a game of Red Light. Others, forming duets, trios, quartets, and choruses, sang one of their favorite songs, to which they now added a new verse.

Light the lights,
Push the buttons
Get the answer exactly.

That we did,
This very day,
And got the answer ac'ratly.

Still others, thinking the occasion called for an entirely new song, made up one that went something like this:

Rabbit, Rabbit, dear fearless Rabbit,
Done led old Dog down a hot trail.
We love Rabbit, dear fearless Rabbit.
Good right down to his little white tail.

215

The frogs played leapfrog, turning somersaults and doing half-twists, three-quarter-twists, and full twists in the air before landing again.

All the others talked comfortably far into the moonlit night, for in spite of the hidden hazards, the uncertainties they each had to cope with, the constant watch they must maintain, the attentiveness they all had to pay to every possible little danger, they knew how to celebrate life, and did so.

When at last everyone started for home, Chipmunk, who was still very excited, said, "In my life whole a good time I've much never had so of and never deserving more of was Rabbit than anyone the Deep Forest Award."